PEACEKEEPER

CHRISTOPHER BRYAN

Diamond Press

Peacekeeper

Christopher Bryan

Printed in the United States of America.

The Diamond Press

Proctors Hall Road

Sewanee, Tennessee

For more information about this book, visit:

www.christopherbryanonline.com

Edition ISBNs

Trade Paperback 978-0-9853911-3-3

e-book 978-0-9853911-4-0

Library of Congress Cataloging-in-Publication data is available upon request.

First Edition 2013

This edition was prepared for printing by The Editorial Department

7650 E. Broadway, #308, Tucson, Arizona 85710

www.editorialdepartment.com

Cover design by Pete Garceau

Book design by Christopher Fisher

Diamond Press logo by Richard Posan for Two Ps

PEACEKEEPER

ONE

Near Tintagel, Cornwall.
Saturday, 25ᵗʰ April, 2009. 11.55 a.m.

It was almost noon, but the skies were dark and there was thunder in the air.

A gleaming black Mercedes S-class limousine moved cautiously down the narrow, rutted lane, its headlights gleaming on wet leaves, grass, and the occasional eye of a small, curious creature. It came to a stop in shadows by an almost concealed gate and there idled for several minutes. Then the wipers were stilled and the headlights dimmed. After another few seconds the engine ceased.

Now there was only the sound of the wind, gusting and sighing through the branches.

"I think this is it, sir," the chauffeur said through the intercom. "I'm afraid I can't get you any closer to the front door. But at least it seems to have stopped raining."

"The car boot," the man in the back said. "You can open it from where you sit?"

"Yes sir. The control's here on the dashboard. Do you want me to open it for you, sir?"

"No, not yet. Listen carefully. You will wait here for me while I go to the cottage—perhaps an hour, perhaps more. When I return, you will remain seated while you open the boot for me and I place some equipment in it. I will not need assistance. Then when I close the boot and get back into the car, you will drive me back to London. Is all that clear?"

"Yes, sir. Perfectly clear, sir. I stay here. I open the boot from here when you say so. And when you've finished and get back in the limo, I drive you back to London."

"Correct. Now wait."

The man got out of the limousine, closed the door, and stood for a moment.

The downpour had indeed stopped, but rain threatened again at any moment. He could hear thunder and it was not, he thought, far away. He looked around him. To tell the truth, leaden skies suited him. All things die, sooner or later, and dark clouds spoke more realistically of such a universe than did the jovial pleasantries of sunshine and blue skies.

And he was in favor of realism, was he not?

He turned toward the cottage.

As he started forward a small dog darted out from the ditch and barked at him—lip curled, eyes bright with fury, barring his approach—then made off, as if answering a sudden call, to disappear in long grass.

The man hesitated only a moment before continuing through the gate and along an untidy path toward the front door.

The woman who answered it looked tired.

"Yes?" she said. "What do you want?"

"I am the chairman," he said. "I wrote to you. I am chairman of the academy."

"Oh yes," she said. "The *new* chairman. They come and they go. The last one wanted to destroy the galaxy."

"He overstepped himself. He achieved nothing."

"And now you want to use the cave."

"Yes."

"Why?"

"I would create servants."

She gazed at him.

He was tall and gray-haired, with a bearing that might have been described as soldierly, even distinguished, and piercing eyes that most people could not meet. His English was perfect to the point of pedantry — perfect in just such a way as to suggest that English was not his mother tongue.

The woman looked into his eyes and seemed unimpressed.

"Be careful what you want," she said. "It's not been used for ninety years."

"I know."

"And then," she said, "it made a servant that finally killed its master and sixty-five million others with him."

"I know. I was there."

The woman stared at him. Then she nodded.

"So you were," she said. "I recognize you now." She considered him again. "You have the ointment?" she said at last.

"I have it."

"How did you get it?"

"A consultant supplied it. He has advised me on its use."

"And you have a purpose for these servants?"

"I..." The tall man hesitated. For the first time he seemed slightly disconcerted. Then he said, "My consultant and I, we have a plan."

The woman shrugged but said no more. Instead she signaled him to wait, went for a cape, then led him around to the back of the cottage and down through the woods. They made their way along an overgrown path past stinging nettles, docks, and brambles, alongside a stream and out at last onto a bluff. The rocks on the left fell away into a valley and the stream splashed down them over a tumble of stones, leaves, and dead branches. On the right the rocks rose steeply but were still suitable for climbing.

"Up there." She pointed. "Follow the path. You'll find it easily enough. It can always be found by those who look for it. And do not come to me again."

Two

The same. A few minutes later.

The tall man crossed the stream by rough steppingstones, avoided a mass of stinging nettles, then wound his way up under an overhanging rock. There, narrow and dark, was the mouth of the cave. It seemed to him that he might easily have missed it if he had not been told that it was there. But then, as the woman said, it was to be found by those who looked for it.

He entered. Within a few paces there was darkness, but he was prepared for that. He produced a small, powerful flashlight whose beam spilled forward, leading him down by narrow passages until at last he came to a natural chamber that echoed with the drip, drip of falling water. A rough stone table stood at the center. He laid the flashlight on it, angled so as to illuminate what he had to do. Then he produced from his pocket a tiny canister, laid that too on the table, and began.

Just *what* he began would have been hard to say. He hummed: a low tone that was at first scarcely audible and then, with no apparent increase in volume, caught some echo or vibration in the cave and seemed to take on a life of its own, bouncing from rock to rock, from floor to ceiling. Meaningless, tuneless, key-less, it filled the cavern, from crack to crevice, low at first, then louder and louder.

The tall man worked with his hands, adding to the dust he scratched from the rough-hewn surface of the table a little ointment from the canister, then a little spittle, then more dust, his fingers always working, smoothing, twisting, kneading. The tuneless tone grew in volume and intensity, vibrating around him until it was clear that he was no longer its source. Now his hands seemed to take on a life beyond human possibility, molding, twisting, kneading, faster than the eye could follow. Between his moving palms something was growing and moving. Shapeless at first, in time it rounded, then lengthened, then swelled with pale protuberances that stretched and grew in turn, twisting and vibrating with a rhythm that balanced and repeated his.

"Ah!"

Abruptly he let the thing go so that it writhed alone upon the table, still twisting and stretching and growing. He stepped back a pace and raised his joined hands above his head, their shadow looming monstrous on the cave walls. He paused. For a moment he was still while the thing writhed before him. Then with a swift chopping motion he dashed his hands upon it, striking at its midpoint. So quick and violent was the blow, it was not at first apparent what had happened — for still the thing writhed and grew, and again his hands moved with it faster than the eye could follow.

Then the purpose of his violence became clear, for his hands separated, each working now on the thing it touched, and the thing itself was now divided, each of two parts twisting and swelling. New protuberances grew at the end of each, bulging and yielding under his working fingers into the rough shape of heads: eyes, noses, the slits of mouths. The limbs of each began to flail, stretching and growing into hands, feet, even fingers and toes of a sort. Then, in a moment, all was still. The vibrating tone ceased.

He stepped back, breathless. The work had taken its toll. He was perspiring freely, and his heart was pounding. He put out a hand to the table to steady himself, and so stood, gasping.

Only after several minutes was he was recovered enough to focus again on what lay before him: twin dolls, each about the height of an average twelve-year-old.

He nodded.

Bending solemnly over them, he pressed dry lips to the mouths of each in turn and kissed them deeply, his tongue questing, seeking. At the end of each kiss he drew back and took a deep breath; then, bending over them, he sighed, and breathed into them.

Again he stood back. He watched. Again tuneless vibration filled the cave, but this time the dull note was matched with a high, sharp tone that pierced thought. Again the creatures were twitching.

Then their eyes opened.

They sat up—first one, then the other—and gazed into the eyes of their creator.

"I am your master," he said. "I am the chairman."

The creatures nodded.

"You will serve me."

Again they nodded.

Leaning forward, he lifted each in turn from the stone table, lowered it to the floor, and set it upright. Then, taking them by the hand and walking between them, he led them out of the chamber back the way he had come toward the cave mouth.

Outside, the clouds were darker than ever, and it was raining heavily. Tree branches tossed and sighed in sudden gusts of wind, the sky echoed with thunder, and flashes of lightning flickered against the gloom.

The tall man stood at the cave mouth for a moment, watching.

Then he and his creatures walked out into the storm.

THREE

Detective Inspector Cecilia Anna Maria Cavaliere's mobile was barking.

"Damn," she said, and pulled it from the pocket of her jeans. "DI Cavaliere here."

"Sergeant Wyatt here, ma'am. Sorry to bother you, but there's been a rather nasty death by violence, and I'm afraid it's in your patch. The DCS knew it was your day off, but he needs you to go there now and take over as senior investigating officer."

Cecilia sighed. Of course the detective chief superintendent was paying her a compliment. Usually Devon and Cornwall police assign detective superintendents rather than mere detective inspectors to such crimes. Still, at this precise moment, just as she was sitting down to Mama's *prima colazione*, it was a compliment she could have done without.

"Where?"

"Weirfield Path, ma'am. Cumberland House. Fellow found dead in his flat."

"Bottom of Colleton Hill? On the corner?"

"That's it, ma'am."

It was one of a number of older buildings beside the River

Exe that had been renovated and converted into fairly classy apartments in the eighties.

"And we're sure this *is* a death by violence?"

"Well of course they didn't touch anything, ma'am, but I gather there's a dead body of a young fellow on a bed with a hole in his throat and a lot of blood about."

"Oh. Well, that sounds fairly conclusive. All right, who's down there so far?"

"PCs Wilkins and Jarman went in answer to the original 999 call, ma'am. DS Jones is there from CID and PCs Jewell and Langdon from uniform. DS Robbin is on his way. And they've sent two scene-of-crime officers—Doctor Foss and Doctor Gibbings. That's going to have to do it for the moment, ma'am. What with all the other stuff, we're a bit short-handed, as you know."

"Never mind. Those'll be fine. Tell them I'll be there as soon as I can get myself together and the morning traffic allows. DS Jones is in charge until I arrive. She can call me if she needs to."

"You've got it, ma'am."

Everybody was talking American these days.

She put the phone down. Papa and Mama were looking at her inquiringly.

"Sorry," she said, "I'm afraid the rest of the morning's just been shot."

She looked at the plate Mama had just set in front of her. In the matter of *prima colazione,* Mama was a convert to the English way: *colazione all'inglese* was better, she said, for the English climate. And indeed, what she had prepared looked perfect, the eggs deep orange and white, the bacon pink and juicy. A loaf of bread still warm (she and Papa had been sent out earlier to walk the dogs and to collect it from the baker in Magdalen Road), sweet butter, and Mama's homemade Seville marmalade were at hand.

"Oh, Mama!" she said.

Figaro (her dog) thumped his tail mournfully. Tocco and Pu (her parents' dogs) looked appropriately depressed.

"Never mind, *bella*," Mama said. "You go and solve your death by violence and Papa and I and Figaro and Tocco and Pu will eat your share. Nothing will be wasted."

Cecilia grimaced. It was not exactly the consolation she'd have chosen. She cut herself a piece of soft, warm bread, spread it liberally with butter, added a generous dollop of Mama's marmalade, and took a bite.

"Mmm, lovely," she said, "but I'm afraid this *boccone* will have to do me for now."

She wiped her mouth, kissed her parents, scratched Figaro behind his ears, patted Tocco and Pu, and then departed for the murder scene, not forgetting to take with her the rest of her bread and marmalade.

FOUR

The one who called himself "consultant" to the academy always arrived in a black 1931 Rolls Royce limousine. And there it was, parked in front of the academy's headquarters when the chairman arrived. So he was not surprised when he opened the door to his office and found the consultant already there, seated in the chairman's own chair behind the chairman's own desk, drumming his fingers.

As usual, the temperature in the ornate, over-furnished room was stifling. Although the clouds had broken and there was sunshine outside, heavy curtains were drawn against the light. The room's only illumination was provided by a couple of low wattage green and gold table lamps and a huge fire, whose flames cast leaping lights and shadows across the walls and ceiling.

The chairman entered and closed the door behind him. His visitor began the conversation without preamble.

"So you've just had a young man killed?"

With anyone else the chairman might have been surprised that he knew so much so soon, but he had long since ceased being surprised by how much the consultant seemed to know. So he merely shrugged.

"Yes," he said. "It is not important."

"Why?"

"Why is it not important?"

"Why did you have him killed?"

"He insulted me."

The consultant stared.

"He insulted *us*. He criticized the academy."

Still the consultant stared.

"He was arrogant. Clever. He laughed at me publicly and he threatened us with ridicule."

"And so?"

"So I wanted him dead!"

The consultant nodded. "Ah, you *wanted* it. *Hoc volo, sic jubeo, sit pro ratione voluntas.* Excellent. And you enjoy the thought of it? All that youth and cleverness and having the nerve to find *you* amusing, now smashed and ruined — you enjoy that?"

"Yes."

"Of course you do." The consultant nodded and seemed to consider. "Still," he said, "it wasn't wise."

"They cannot possibly trace it here."

"Perhaps those who investigate will be more clever than you think. He did have a connection here."

"I had someone arrange for him to be killed away from here, in another city, and I had them use an *instrument* for the killing, an oaf — he knows nothing. As for the young man's connection with us, he had many connections with many people. Why should the police suspect this one rather than others nearer at hand? They will pay attention to what is obvious. They always do."

The consultant shook his head. "Perhaps they will. Perhaps they won't. Still, it wasn't wise. But —" he held up his hand as the chairman seemed about to argue, "it is done and it cannot be undone. We have more important things to discuss. The androids — you followed my instructions?"

"Of course."

"And it worked. They live."

"Yes. It was almost… *supernatural*."

"But there is no supernatural, is there? That's what you say, isn't it? I've shown you how to tap into natural forces — the life force, the élan vital. That is all, is it not?"

"Of course."

"Believing in gods and devils and such nonsense, that was the folly of your predecessor."

"It was."

The consultant nodded. "I'm delighted to find you so clear and consistent in your views. Now as to the androids, I'll take them with me. I have a man who will program them. Then they can be returned to you and you'll play with them for a little. We'll definitely need a field test — I'm sure you'll enjoy that."

The chairman smiled.

The consultant nodded.

"Of course you will. And now I must go. I have work to do in the City. Try to control your desire to kill, just for the present, will you? It's not that I've anything against it, you understand. Just that for the moment I think a little restraint might be wise. And in the meantime, I'll be sending you a new client. If he's half the man I think he is, he'll be highly amusing to us both."

FIVE

The Topsham Road. 9.00 a.m.

Cecilia first went back to her own house, which was next door to her parents. It had been their wedding present to her, although she'd now been living in it alone for something over two years—ever since her husband left her. She changed her clothes, collected things she would need for the day, and set off.

She had been right to warn Sergeant Wyatt that the morning traffic might delay her. It was heavy. Heavier than usual, it seemed, although Exeter always seemed to be busy these days. Of course she *could* turn on flashing lights and the siren and have everything scatter before her, but that temptation she rejected with conscious virtue. The corpse couldn't get any deader, there were thoroughly competent officers already at the scene, and nothing was to be gained by her causing a disturbance in order to show up ten minutes sooner than she would turn up without causing a disturbance.

The red MGB in front of her came to a juddering halt at the traffic lights as they turned red—and remained there when they turned green.

Back in the traffic line, cars and trucks started to hoot.

Oh, Lord! This she could really have done without.

So now she did turn on the flashing blue lights, though not the siren. The lights were visible way back in the traffic line and at least persuaded people to shut up. Then she unfastened her seat belt, got out, and went to the MG.

"Aw, hell, I've been here less than a month and already I've gotten in trouble with the police!" The young man was wearing a seersucker jacket. Obviously American. Military, she suspected. "I'm real sorry, ma'am, it's just gone dead on me."

"You do seem to be in a bit of trouble, sir, but not with the police." Cecilia smiled at him. "Why don't we get you to the side of the road out of the traffic? Then we can let all these people through and decide what to do next."

"Oh, sure. Yes ma'am!"

He got out quickly and started to push, one hand on the steering wheel.

"It'll be easier if you take the handbrake off, sir."

"Ma'am, you must think I'm a complete idiot."

"Just a bit overexcited, sir! Mind the curb as you push her in, it's a bit steep just there. You don't want to spoil your paintwork. Good. Wait for me here, please."

Though to be sure, there wasn't much else he could do.

She went back to the police car and parked in front of the MG. She got the traffic moving again, then turned back to the young man.

"Do you have your license, sir? You're not in trouble, but I am supposed to check it."

"Yes, ma'am. Sure. Here, ma'am."

She glanced at it. It was pretty much as she expected.

"Welcome to Britain, Captain Scott, and welcome to Exeter. I see you're stationed at R.A.F. Harlsden."

"Yes, ma'am."

Cecilia knew exactly what that meant. Her Majesty's government did not boast about the United States' missile sites on its soil, but ever since the 1958 US-UK Mutual Defense Agreement they had existed nonetheless, discreetly described as "Royal

Air Force" bases and protected by R.A.F. police. Harlsden was one of them.

She looked again at the car. It was quite like the MG Papa used to have when she was little, and still (she suspected) rather regretted not having any longer.

"Does the motor turn over when you try to start it?"

"No ma'am. I stalled at the lights—I've only just bought her and I guess I'm not used to the shift yet. But now when I try to start her again she's dead as a duck. Nothing."

She nodded. "Open the bonnet," she said.

"Ma'am?"

She smiled. "The hood, sir. Would you open it?"

"Oh, sure. Yes, ma'am."

She peered in. The engine was filthy, including the battery connections—one of which looked loose. She twisted and pressed it, making as firm a connection as she could.

"Try again."

He turned the ignition key. Immediately the engine turned over and fired.

"Ma'am, that's fantastic. Are all English policewomen as brilliant as you?"

"Oh yes, sir," she said. "It's a requirement. Look, unless you do something about it the car will die on you again. You've got a loose battery connection and you need to get it replaced. You've also got a dirty engine. I'd get it cleaned and serviced straight away if I were you, and make sure they deal with those battery connections. That's a nice car. When I was little my papa had one just like it."

"I'll do that, ma'am, believe me. I'll do it. And thank you *very* much."

"Don't mention it, sir. Drive carefully. And have a good day."

"Thank you, ma'am. You too!"

She returned to the police car.

He wasn't really her type and she loathed seersucker.

But she couldn't deny he was a charmer.

Nice taste in cars, too.

She looked at her watch.

The delay had cost her a good fifteen minutes, so she'd better be getting on.

But she still wasn't going to turn on the siren.

Six

A few minutes later.

Cecilia drove down Colleton Hill and parked near the bottom, twenty or so meters from Cumberland House. Various police vehicles with their distinctive blue and yellow Battenberg markings were parked in front of the building. A white science-and-tech van was close by. A constable stood at the door to one of the ground floor flats. Crime-scene tape cordoned off the visitors' car park, the garden, and the residents' car park at the rear. Two figures in white looking vaguely like spacemen and carrying plastic bags emerged, had a word with the constable, then trudged on with their burdens towards the van.

She got out of the car.

The sky was overcast, but just then a sudden break in the clouds let shafts of sunlight through. A breeze ruffled the water, breaking it into pinpricks of light. A swan was taking off just above the entrance to the canal. Even from where she stood she could hear the beat of its wings and the rhythmic plash as its feet drove into the water. Then in an instant it was aloft, gliding upwards in apparently effortless silence.

The constable was waving at her to come through. It was PC Wilkins. She liked young Wilkins, who seemed to enjoy everything. He reminded her of Lazarus, the large and enthusi-astic dog they'd had when she was little.

"I see you're having a busy day," she said.

"Yes, ma'am. PC Jarman and me, we were first on the scene."

At which point DS Verity Jones appeared behind him. DS Jones — secretly known to Cecilia as little Miss Perfect, thanks to her disconcerting habit of looking immaculately groomed at all times and in all places, whatever she was doing and however long she'd been doing it. Today she was a vision in powder blue: very elegant and fetching, only the plastic gloves strik-ing a slightly incongruous note. But Cecilia wasn't deceived. She'd discovered some time ago that little Miss Perfect also had a logical mind, a first from Oxford in *Litterae Humaniores*, good detective instincts, and no fear whatever of hard work.

"Good morning, Detective Sergeant," Cecilia said, reaching into her shoulder bag for a pair of plastic gloves.

"Good morning, ma'am," Verity Jones said, matching Cecilia's formality.

Cecilia pulled on the gloves. "You seem to have everything under control."

"Thank you ma'am. The SOCOs have had their initial onceover, as you see. But they'd still like us to tread only where they've shown me."

"All right. So why don't you show me what's to be seen, then tell me what there is to tell so far?"

"Yes ma'am." Verity led her from the tiny hall through a doorway on the left and into a larger room. "Well, obviously, this is the sitting room."

Cecilia looked around. A television stand with no television. Otherwise everything was much as one would expect.

She nodded.

"And through here, ma'am, this is a spare bedroom he seems to have been using as a study."

Cecilia peered at the shelves. Poetry. Some nineteenth-century novels. Trollope. The Brontes. Several Arden Shakespeares. A school edition of Chaucer's *Knight's Tale*. A two-volume *Shorter Oxford Dictionary*. Some CDs. Handel. Vivaldi. Corelli.

She looked at the desk. A pile of papers at the side. A few more on the floor. She bent and looked at the paper on top. "'Bottom the weaver has been closer to the centre of this wonderful and mysterious play than any other of its characters...' Discuss." Question marks and corrections in the margins in red. The center of the desk was empty save for what looked like a computer cord coming from the back, and a British Telecom router. But there was no computer.

Again Cecilia nodded.

"Dining-kitchenette, ma'am."

Cecilia glanced around and grimaced. Too small. It would be hell to try to cook seriously in here.

"And this, ma'am, is the bedroom."

It smelled of blood.

Chairs overturned. A tabletop cracked. Pictures askew. Lampstand on the ground. A full-length mirror shattered. And on the bed, face up, the sprawled figure of a young man wearing pajamas, in his neck a gaping wound from which crimson had spread in every direction.

Cecilia sighed. "God help us," she said softly.

"Yes, ma'am," Verity said quietly.

There was a pause.

"His name is John Stewart Cox and he was teaching English at Exmouth Community College."

Cecilia surveyed the scene intently for several more minutes.

"All right."

"Bathroom and loo, ma'am."

There were splashes of red in the bathroom sink. She raised an eyebrow and looked at Verity Jones, who simply met her gaze. There was a towel on the floor. Cecilia bent and touched it with the back of her hand, pulling back the plastic glove. The towel was wet.

"Right," Cecilia said, "let's go outside and you can fill me

in. Good morning," she added, seeing the scene-of-crime officers who had returned from putting whatever it was into their
van and were now standing in the hallway. "Dr. Foss and Dr.
Gibbings, when you go over the sink in the bathroom and the
wet towel, make sure you check in the u-pipe *under* the sink,
won't you? It looks as though the killer washed in there, so the
grunge and grot may be informative."

Gibbings smiled. "We noticed. We'll see to it."

"Good. I thought you would."

She and Verity went and sat in her car. The break in the clouds
had vanished and the sky now threatened more rain, but still
the air from the river was fresh and sweet and she opened the
windows.

"Okay Verity, what've we got?"

"Well, ma'am, from our point of view it started at seven
thirty-five a.m. when the victim's sister, Mary Cox, called it in
on her mobile."

"Mary Cox?"

"Yes ma'am. Do you know her?"

"I know of *a* Mary Cox. Maybe she's not the same one.
Anyway, we can sort that out later. Go on."

"Well, ma'am, she said she's been phoning her kid brother
every morning at seven to make sure he doesn't oversleep and
be late for work. This morning he didn't answer and didn't
answer so finally she got on her bike and cycled down here a
bit before half past seven. She found the door to the flat open,
which surprised her, so of course she went in and, well, you've
seen it. She says she saw the place was a mess and thought
something terrible must have happened and that's why she
called us."

"And you believe her?"

"Yes, ma'am, except I rather think she went into the bedroom and saw him. So far everything she says checks out, and
if she's lying she's a good actress, which of course she may be.
But I tend to believe her."

"Okay. So what then?"

"Well, following the 999 call they sent a patrol car with PCs Jarman and Wilkins to the flat. They found Mary Cox in a distressed state, sitting on the bench over there"—she gestured toward the river walk—"with her mobile phone still in her hand. PC Wilkins stayed with her while PC Jarman went in, saw that the victim was dead, secured the crime scene, and sent for us. While the SOCOs collected evidence I sat on the bench and talked with Mary Cox. When I thought I'd more or less got her story straight, I managed to persuade her to let them take her to the station, and I assume you'll want to talk to her there yourself. So far she's our only witness."

"Good. Verity, you're doing fine. All of you are. You carry on here, and I'll go and interview Mary Cox." She looked at her watch. "Let's meet in my office at, say, ten forty-five, and compare notes."

"Yes ma'am."

SEVEN

George Jameson sat alone in the cellar of Gordon's Wine Bar, gazing gloomily at the glass of Chivas Regal in front of him.

At a table at the other end of the cellar a knot of young Americans were laughing and talking volubly and loudly.

He wished they'd shut up.

It didn't help his mood that in a way he was in their debt. A group of American companies was having a conference or convention or some damn thing in the city, and to accommodate them Gordon's was opening this week daily at ten a.m. instead of its usual eleven.

Someone must know someone for that to happen.

After all, it wasn't as if Gordon's needed the business.

Still, it *had* happened, and that was why George could be here at 10.05 in the morning with his Chivas Regal in front of him.

And he really needed it.

So he supposed he owed them.

He sighed and took a swallow of his drink.

He might as well face facts. Under the circumstances, his chances of the partnership at the bank were zero. The problem, of course, was Ruggles — Ruggles with his sickening reputation for integrity and his undoubted ability. If it weren't for Ruggles, George might be looking quite good. He had, after all, managed last year to pull off the exchange of securities with the Swedish conglomerate. But things in the City had changed, and now wheeling and dealing was unfashionable and being steady and having integrity were in. And Ruggles, the self-righteous cretin, was going to —

"May I join you?"

He looked up. "Oh, it's you. Of course." They weren't exactly friends. In fact, he never seemed to see the fellow except in a bar, and usually after his third Chivas Regal.

"So you're drinking early too," George said. "I suppose if one *must* be invaded by colonials one might as well take advantage of it."

The other shrugged. "You look preoccupied," he said.

George snorted. "I suppose you could say that."

Two more Chivas Regals were ordered. Then, without really intending to, he found himself telling. About the bank. About the partnership. About Ruggles.

"So," the man said when he'd finished. "You want this partnership?"

"What do you think? Of course I want it, if only not to see it go to that smug little creep Ruggles."

The other drained his glass, put it down upon the table, and looked at him hard.

Then reached into his inside pocket, brought out a wallet, and produced a card, which he handed to George.

Heavily embossed. Distinctly classy.

The Academy for Philosophical Studies. Scientia Potentia Est.

George examined it curiously, then looked up at the other, who was beckoning to the barman.

"I don't understand," he said when another Chivas Regal had arrived and the barman withdrawn. "Why are you showing me this?"

"I take it then you've not heard of the academy?"

"Not that I know of. Should I?"

"It doesn't matter. It's enough to say that *I* know them quite well. I'm their senior consultant. And they do have certain… *abilities* in these matters."

"Abilities? What kind of abilities?"

"That isn't important for the moment. The question is, how much do you want this partnership?"

George's acquaintance was looking at him—into him, almost—with an intensity that made him uncomfortable. On the other hand, just possibly the fellow really did know something… or this academy knew something… or someone… and George was in a state to clutch at straws.

"I repeat, how much do you want this partnership?"

George tried to inject a note of levity into the proceedings.

"Well," he said, "I don't want it enough to pay for it with my life, if that's what you—"

"What I am saying is, do you want this partnership enough to abandon things that some people think important—justice, honor, common decency—things like that? Do you want it *that* much?"

And now George, who'd left his wife without a qualm when he'd been more attracted by a leggy Swedish blonde, and equally without qualm had dispatched the leggy blonde back to Sweden when he got bored with her, George who was accustomed to swapping jokes about anal sex and cunnilingus without a blush—this same George, at the abrupt mention of justice, honor, and common decency felt himself growing warm. What the devil was the matter with him? Justice and honor, for Christ's sake! What was this? The Middle Ages? He took another sip and again attempted levity.

"Well, you know what they say. All's fair in love and war—and business."

"They say that, do they?" The man nodded. "Well, I'm delighted to hear it. But the point is—you. What do *you* say?"

There was another pause.

The Americans were saying noisy goodbyes to the barman, who was apparently their new best friend.

George took another swallow. He was *really* uncomfortable now. He also desperately, deeply, wanted that partnership.

"*Do* you want it that much?"

He took another drink, then gazed into his glass.

"I suppose I do," he said at last. "As they say, all's fair—"

"Yes, I know. You've already told me what they say." He bent towards George. "Now listen. Ten days from today, when the partners meet—Gordon and Settler's I think you said it was, didn't you?"

George nodded.

"Yes, well, when the partners of Gordon and Settler's have their meeting, ten days from today, they will choose you as the new partner. And you will owe it to the academy. You will be in the academy's debt. Do I make myself clear, George?"

The haze of alcohol cleared abruptly. George had not been aware the man knew his name. And as for being in debt...

"Now wait a minute—"

"No," the other said, abruptly standing. "I don't have any more minutes. For the last time I ask you, do you want this partnership that much? Or not? Be careful how you answer."

George hesitated. The prospect opened before him. The power. The prestige. He would be unstoppable. Those stick-in-the-muds on the board were frightened of what had happened to AIG and all the others. He wasn't. He *understood* finance, for God's sake. First, though, he needed that position. And just suppose, just suppose... this man, this academy, whatever, knew something? About Ruggles, perhaps? Maybe Ruggles wasn't the model of integrity he was cracked up to be?

Damn it, he would *not* miss the chance.

"Yes," he said at last. "I want it that much. But what can you do about it?"

The other smiled.

"As I say. You will be chosen. And you will owe it to the

academy. You may keep the card. And mind your arm! You'll knock your drink over if you aren't careful."

George looked down, made sure his drink was safe, and looked back again toward the other. But the other was gone.

On impulse George left his drink where it was, walked to the steps and so up to the street. He could hear sounds of traffic from the Embankment in one direction and from Charing Cross opposite—the soft hum of London. Villiers Street itself was quiet, almost deserted, surprisingly so for this time of morning.

George stepped out onto the pavement where he could see further. He looked up and down. He walked to the curb and looked again. Nothing. His drinking companion was simply nowhere to be seen.

A vintage 1930s Rolls Royce, monstrous and gleaming black, was pulling away from the curb on the far side of the road. A woman with a dog was coming from the direction of the Strand. There was no one else.

He stared at the Rolls as it passed, but already it was moving quickly and he could not see who was inside.

The Rolls continued up to the end of Villiers Street and then turned right into John Adams Street, disappearing from his view.

He stood for a moment longer, then shook his head, shrugged, and went back down the steps into the cellar.

His drink was waiting for him.

EIGHT

London. John Adams Street, 10.20 a.m.

John Adams Street was by no means deserted, and the inhabitants of that part of London are not notably unobservant. Yet for some reason or other, and with just one exception, no one was paying attention at that precise moment when, just before the black Rolls would have reached the intersection with Buckingham Street, it slowed, shimmered darkly for a moment, and disappeared.

The one exception was standing near to the curb almost exactly opposite where the Rolls vanished — a man of medium height, dark hair touched with gray, dark bearded, a little past his youth. He watched the whole thing. It was almost as if he were expecting it. Then he sighed and shook his head.

At that moment a magazine vendor close by looked up from checking his wares and sniffed. His nose and mouth wrinkled in distaste.

"Ugh! Rotten eggs!" he said.

The man looked across at him and smiled.

"Quite right," he said, speaking with a slight German accent.

When Mary Cox came into the interview room at the Heavitree Road station accompanied by a woman PC, she looked tired and upset and was paler than when Cecilia had last seen her, but Cecilia recognized the young woman at once. Mary Cox was first violinist and leader for the British Concert, an internationally acclaimed chamber orchestra. Cecilia and her parents had heard them perform only a few days earlier at a concert in the cathedral. Mary Cox had played the solo in the third movement—the melancholy musette—of Handel's Concerto Grosso in G Minor, and then the solo for Vivaldi's Violin Concerto in D Major. And she'd played them as well as Cecilia had ever heard them played.

After some time with a counselor and several cups of tea, Ms. Cox was evidently more coherent than she'd been earlier. She seemed a pleasant, quiet young woman. When Cecilia referred to her talent as a musician, she was modest—indeed, seemed quite surprised that Cecilia even knew who she was.

The story of her part in the morning's events remained essentially the same as that relayed by Verity Jones, except she now said plainly that when she got to her brother's flat she'd gone to the bedroom door and seen him.

"I'm sorry, officer, I should have said that sooner. I know it was foolish of me. It's just that, at first—I couldn't say it. I just couldn't say it."

As she listened, Cecilia was aware how much she did not want Mary Cox to be guilty of her brother's murder, not only because she was a brilliant violinist but also because she found herself liking her. That awareness made her cautious. What we can't show, we don't know. Given where Mary Cox had passed the night and her knowledge of her brother's flat, quite clearly she'd had both means and opportunity to have murdered him. And for all Cecilia knew, given the antagonisms and hatreds that can lurk within families, perhaps she'd also had motive.

Mary Cox was entirely cooperative. She agreed without hesitation to the interview's being videoed—a procedure that was, as Cecilia always pointed out, as much a means of checking on the police as on the witness. She willingly provided fingerprints,

prints of her shoes (which she said were the ones she'd worn in the apartment), and a DNA sample. At the conclusion of the interview Cecilia determined that for the time being Mary Cox should be given the benefit of the doubt. She accepted a ride back to her apartment in a police car, along with the condolences of the police and the proviso that she keep them informed of her whereabouts until their investigations were complete. This, too, she seemed entirely willing to do — although for as long as she remained with the British Concert it seemed hardly necessary, since the movements of one of the best known chamber orchestras in the world were hardly a secret. And the truth was, despite Cecilia's professional determination not to be persuaded by feelings, she did think the young violinist was telling the truth. Certainly she didn't look like a murderer.

But then, what does a murderer look like?

NINE

The outskirts of the infernal city.

In the rear of the Rolls, the consultant made a note in his Filofax, then sat back and allowed himself to relax. George Jameson of the wine bar was, it seemed, comfortably in hand. There was nothing to worry about there. His gaze roamed casually over the car's interior and rested for a moment on his driver, a gray-clad figure upright behind the enormous old-fashioned steering wheel. Beyond him, through the windscreen, the sounds and sunshine of London had vanished, to be replaced by… well… by nothing much: a gray, largely featureless landscape, much of it blanketed in fog. Here and there he could see houses, some of them large and at first sight imposing, though with little relationship to each other or anything around them. The Rolls progressed, and in time there were more buildings, most of them apparently derelict, and even a few shops, though they appeared to be closed. A couple of dimly lit entrances opened into what looked like seedy nightclubs, from which strains of tinny music could be heard.

And everywhere, patches of fog.

These were the suburbs of the infernal city.

Now he could see figures in the streets, some wandering, some standing still. They were not so much people as the remnants of people, varying in appearance from the relatively solid (just a little blurred at the edges) to the near transparent (in effect, ghosts). Most were solitary. A few were in conversation, though their conversations seldom lasted long. Their faces were generally haggard, haunted as by something within that defiled and devoured them. They seemed to be disintegrating even as he watched, and they muttered endlessly, a jumble of mumbled words and half-formed thoughts.

"It's not fair... it was their fault... she betrayed me... all I ask... all I want... all I've done... I want my rights... he deserves to suffer... they're just a pair of faggots... it isn't right... over-sexed little tart... it was their fault... I've done nothing illegal... he's to blame... all I want..."

The consultant nodded and sat back. It was as he expected.

Such the litany of hell.

Such its citizens.

Of many cultures and races, of many faiths and none, for hell, like heaven, is nothing if not ecumenical.

Some had once been great, at least as the world counts greatness: financiers whose greed cost the jobs and livelihoods of thousands, a tyrant who'd murdered his own people, an elected leader who'd lied to his fellow-citizens so as to lead them into a needless war.

Others had garnered no attention at all. Through relatively uneventful lives they'd merely gone with the flow, always careful to pay lip service to duty and compassion even as they never allowed such notions to influence anything they actually did. Gracious to the powerful, they'd indulged in malice only when it was safe to do so.

One thing, however, was common to all. They had arrived here confident in their own rectitude, content with what they had made of themselves. Whatever had gone wrong with their lives, whatever the fallout, it had never been their fault. Others, or perhaps even life itself, had failed them.

Any who were *not* so confident or content—any who were

inclined to admit past failings or to blame themselves for things that had gone wrong with their lives, any who had the faintest hope or even longing to be something better than they now were—all such as that were, of course, unfit for citizenship in the infernal city, and would not be admitted.

ABANDON ALL HOPE, YOU THAT ENTER.

The Florentine poet had rightly observed what was written over the gates to the city. He had observed, but he had not understood. He supposed the words to be a threat. A warning.

They were of course nothing of the kind.

They were the condition of entry.

TEN

Seated in Cecilia's office, Verity Jones spread out her notes. "You saw the crime scene, ma'am. Given the broken furniture and the fresh bruises on the victim's face, it looks as if he put up a fight. And now we've got two witnesses from a flat in the next building, a couple who say shouts and sounds of a fight woke them up at about three a.m., which would fit with forensics' estimate of the time of death."

"Didn't think of calling the police, I suppose?"

"They said they thought it was just someone's television."

"Oh, great!"

"Well, ma'am, on preliminary examination Cox looks to have been killed by being stabbed in the throat with a pair of scissors we found on the floor by the bed—which Mary Cox says she's pretty sure were his. In other words it looks as if he was killed with a weapon from the scene."

"Which suggests the killer only meant to rob the place."

Verity nodded.

"How do we think the killer got in? Mary Cox said the door was normally locked."

"We found a window at the back partly open with every sign it had been forced, which would point to its being a stranger rather than someone who could get in easily."

"Yes. Unless someone who could get in easily made it look like that. I think Mary Cox is telling the truth, but I'm not ruling her out yet."

"Yes, ma'am. Still, if she did do it she's quite clever, because she not only made the window look as if it had been forced, she also planted a penknife in the flower urn just outside the window, with a notch in it that looks exactly as if it was used to do the forcing."

"No fingerprints on it, I suppose?"

"Not a chance. Even the stupidest criminal knows to wear gloves these days."

"If only we'd never told detective-story writers about fingerprints! We labor under cruel disadvantages, Verity."

"Yes, ma'am." Verity grinned. "Anyway, I'm getting them to check out the back for footprints and fingerprints this afternoon, just in case. Thank goodness the rain's holding off. It's been threatening all day."

"The penknife's not traceable, I suppose."

"Common as dirt, ma'am. You could buy one almost anywhere."

"All right," Cecilia said, "so, assuming for the sake of argument that Mary Cox isn't a brilliant actress with a penchant for faking evidence, we might suppose the killer was a stranger who couldn't gain entry by the front door."

"Exactly. But in that case I think the killer probably *left* by the front door. Which would make a lot of sense. There's stuff missing."

Cecilia had guessed as much when she saw the empty television stand and the empty desk.

"Mary Cox says there should be a nearly new flat-screen Samsung thirty-two-inch television and a Dell Inspiron laptop and a box with money in it. She reckons about a hundred quid."

"A few hundred quid altogether. And a young man dies for it."

Verity nodded. "Still, ma'am, it'd account for the killer

leaving by the front door. You'd not want to go out through that window carrying a thirty-two-inch television."

"And I suppose it would explain the door being unlocked. You wouldn't have a hand free to lock it as you left, then once you'd got clear you'd be anxious to get the hell out of there rather than go back and shut it properly."

"Exactly. So on the face of it, it looks as if what we have is a burglary gone bad."

"On the face of it, yes." Cecilia frowned. "I'm not sure it *quite* adds up. Why would the burglar have thought the place was empty anyway? It seems an odd place to choose for a surreptitious break-in. What about other evidence?"

"Well, ma'am, they're working on it. Tomorrow's the day for Cox's cleaner, lucky for us because it means the place is quite dusty. They're checking for shoe impressions, fingerprints — you never know, we might get lucky — and there are some blood samples on the carpet as well as the other stuff you noticed in the bathroom. The coroner's taken charge of the body and of course there'll be the post mortem and an inquest. And we'll keep a general eye out for the TV and the laptop. Luckily Mary Cox knew where he kept the serial numbers of both."

"Good."

"We did find one other thing, ma'am. It was on the victim's dressing table with some other cards, for local restaurants and takeaways. But this one I thought you should see."

Cecilia took the card.

As was her habit, Verity Jones had saved the best until last.

Heavily embossed. Definitely expensive. *The Academy for Philosophical Studies. Scientia Potentia Est.*

Cecilia's heart began to race.

"Good grief!"

"Yes, ma'am. I thought you'd be interested."

What Verity Jones knew was that Cecilia had been interested in the academy some time ago, when it kept appearing on the fringe of a number of mysterious deaths.

What Verity did not know was how much Cecilia had learned later about the academy. That they had tried to kill her parents and sought to perform a rite whose destructive powers were apparently without limit. That at Cranston College in London she and her parents, their friend Michael Aarons the priest, and a young scientist called Charlie Brown had been led to confrontation with a deadly power unleashed by the academy. And that Charlie had given his life to stop it.

None of this was the stuff of police reports or the Crown Prosecution Service, none of it was likely to be credible to those who'd had no part in it, and Cecilia had perforce kept it to herself. But now she wondered.

Was this just a robbery gone bad?

"For the moment, ma'am," Verity said, "I'm just going to treat the academy like we would anyone else in London. Ask the Met to call on them. Normal inquiries, normal channels. We found their card, so what was the victim's connection with them? See what they say. Is that all right?"

Cecilia hesitated. She'd asked a couple of colleagues in the Met to keep an eye on the place some time ago, though none of them had any idea what she knew.

"Tell you what, Verity, let me follow up on the academy. I was thinking of going up to town this afternoon anyway. I'll pay them a call and see what they say. You and the others handle the rest. I'll let you know what I find."

"Oh. All right, ma'am."

Cecilia bit her lip. What she'd just said was what she rather thought her friend Michael Aarons would call an evasion. It was true, she'd thought about going up to town to look at the shops on her day off. She'd thought about it several days ago, and she'd decided against it. The fact was, she'd just been about to offer to take Verity Jones to an early lunch.

But at sight of the card from the Academy for Philosophical Studies, she'd lost her appetite.

ELEVEN

The Infernal City.

The Rolls gained speed. They continued downhill through mostly mean streets, leveling out as they crossed the massive suspension bridge that spanned the Abyss, and then downhill again on a wide road through the ten middle districts of the city. At last they came to Central Administration, an impressive set of buildings overlooking Lake Cocytus, whose orange and yellow flames leaped and flickered in vivid contrast to the gray half-light that pervaded most of the city. Here were the main offices, block upon block filled with scurrying demons — harassed secretaries, anxious clerks, worried administrators; with spreadsheets, strategic plans, and projections; with data bases and computer simulations (Lucifer himself insisted on keeping up with the latest earth technology); with an interlocking and constantly updated system of six hundred and sixty-six committees whose every record was kept in hard copy as well as computer files. Here, in short, was the bureaucracy of hell. Its primary purpose was to maintain itself in what seemed to be activity, thus preserving for those involved the sense that they were doing something even if they didn't know what it was. But that, as Lucifer pointed out, was true of many bureaucracies, even some on earth.

The Rolls came to a halt in front of wide steps, lofty columns, and enormous double doors. The consultant's driver hurried to open the car door for him, bowing low as he emerged.

"It is good to see you again in your glory, lord," he said.

The consultant nodded curtly. The driver was a minor demon and merited no greater acknowledgment. Doubtless, like all demons, in his heart he hated his angelic lord, being cowed only by his power and majesty. Still, what he said was true so far as it went. It was indeed better to be free for a while of the constraints of appearing to be human, constraints that confined his wings and his glory. Here he could be who he was. And was not the maintenance of angelic glory precisely what the Great Rebellion had been about?

He looked up and around at the vast circular valley to whose center he had come, circle upon circle. How much he and the others had achieved since mere self-respect had led them to separate themselves from the One! And how absurdly they had been misrepresented! Here, as any could see, were no horned imps brandishing pitchforks or herding reluctant souls into the flames. Here the inhabitants were simply at liberty to indulge themselves forever in whatever fantasy they chose about them-selves or the universe. Nothing and nobody would challenge them. And no one was here who did not choose to be.

Some on earth claimed that hell was nothing, merely a state of mind. The consultant shook his head. He'd have thought even a human would be intelligent enough to see that hell was real, if only because those who chose it were real. The One claimed to have bestowed that reality on them as a gift in the act of cre-ation. Typical arrogance! The lords of the infernal city naturally rejected such a claim. Their best researchers were working non-stop on formulae that should correctly explain their existence.

Admittedly, hell could not yet *create* reality. The researchers were working on that, too. For the moment, hell could create only illusion. But that, for most of hell's purposes, was per-fectly satisfactory and was indeed in some ways better than reality. It was more flexible. It was more easily adaptable. And it was instant.

And like all things instant, from coffee to sex, it was also bland, tasteless, and boring.

The thought cut into the consultant's consciousness like a blow, unexpected and unsought, then metamorphosed before he could stop it into a cascade of related memories and questions.

Could even he deny that the gray half-light surrounding him was drab and mournful? Even compared to earthly sunlight, even compared to the London he'd just left, let alone when compared to the light of heaven?

The memory of that light never entirely left him. How could it? He had once swum in it as his natural element. In its rays and amid strains of the universal music he had known delight. Compared with that light, the light around him now was darkness. Compared with that music, there was nothing here but cacophony.

Was it any wonder servants of the One called the infernal city a place of torment? Could even the lords of the city deny that those whom they seduced into its citizenship must gradually disintegrate? How could they not? Hell offered them no vision, and where there is no vision, the people perish.

As for the consultant himself and his companions in rebellion, they had seen the glory, and now they did not see it. How could they *not* be tormented? They had settled for a sordid second-rate, while the best—glorious, beautiful, and real—still waited for them.

Was it then too late to turn back?

Have I any pleasure in the death of the wicked, says the Lord God, *and not rather that they should turn from their ways and live?*

NEVER!

The consultant reared up and extended his great wings, hissing with rage. What could possibly bring such thoughts into his mind? That such treasonous ideas could still occasionally haunt him — him, for billions of years a lord of hell — was infuriating, humiliating. Could it be that even now and even here he was not safe from attack by the One? He had heard recently of an angelic lord and rebel, one like himself, who had actually gone back to the enemy. The consultant shuddered. Was nothing truly damned anymore?

He shook his head.

One must focus on the main thing: *on what the rebellion had gained.*

What if the humans they brought into the city did experience certain diminutions of form and capability? Shouldn't that change be seen not as loss but as the clearing away of clutter? Does the butterfly *lose* by sloughing off the chrysalis? In all likelihood this apparent disintegration was simply a first stage in the emergence of new modes of existence in which, untrammelled by flesh, the citizens of hell would be free to evolve beyond mere humanity into new forms of truly *spiritual* being.

And what if the half-light surrounding the infernal city was darkness in comparison with the light they had left? Would that change the fact, which was precisely as one of the One's own servants had stated it: "Light came into the world, and people *preferred* the darkness." Exactly! The sniveling groveler had got it in one!

Admittedly, being a typical groveler, having perceived the fact, he'd then missed the point. He'd blathered on about people's preference being a "verdict" on them, a "judgment." He simply couldn't or wouldn't see that what they'd done — what the city had persuaded them to do — was to *assert their freedom.* They'd defied destiny. And in the light of that stark, virile defiance each resident of the infernal city, fallen angel and damned and disintegrating human alike, could make the same proud boast: *I did it my way.*

A clang.

The consultant looked up, distracted from his reverie. The great double doors had opened. There seemed to be some minor commotion within. Then from between them emerged a clerk carrying a file, another demon, who bowed low as he approached.

"My lord! I have the report you requested. I believe we've found someone who'll meet your requirements."

The consultant took the file and scanned through details about a superintendent of police serving in southwest England.

"I remember this one," he said. "I worked on him myself once, some earth years ago. It was I who set him on the path. I see two of your agents, junior tempters, are working on him now."

"Yes, my lord."

The consultant looked back again at the file.

"I don't like the look of the wife. You should never have let him get involved with a woman like that. Big mistake."

"She *is* a disappointment, my lord."

"Otherwise he seems well enough suited. And I see he doesn't listen to his wife."

"No, my lord."

The consultant nodded again, and closed the file.

"Then he will do," he said. "Tell your agents they are relieved of duty. I'll take charge of this case myself."

"Yes, my lord. And if I may say so, my lord, I'm sure it could not be in safer hands."

TWELVE

R.A.F. Harlsden. 2.00 p.m.

L ance Scott eased the MG forward to the barricade, and took it out of gear. Despite that breakdown early on at the stop-lights in Exeter—in some ways as a result of it—he'd had a suc-cessful day. He'd taken the beautiful policewoman's advice. His landlady had given him the address of an auto repair shop she trusted, and as luck would have it they'd had a cancellation that same morning.

So the MG had been checked and serviced, the engine cleaned until it gleamed, and the battery connections replaced while he sat in a coffee shop and read the latest Tom Clancy. He'd still been in time to pick up David as planned, and the MG was now running like a dream. He was actually getting used to the shift—even beginning to relish the peculiar sense of closeness to the engine and the road it gave him. Above all he was rel-ishing the fact that he now owned the car he'd wanted all his life—ever since he was a kid, when he'd seen one on television in an old British B movie the name of which he couldn't even remember.

He'd thought Sophie would laugh when he told her about it on the phone last night, or wonder why on earth he'd want an old car. But she'd surprised him, just as she so often did. "Good for you, Lance," she'd said. "I hope you'll take me for a ride in it." And her voice was soft.

Here was the R.A.F. policeman.

"Good morning, sergeant. Captain Lancelot Scott and Lieutenant James Levi. 92nd Missile Wing. United States Air Force."

"Good morning, sir!"

Of course the man knew perfectly well who they were, since they'd met him earlier when Gianni Turso, a brother officer, brought them through on their orientation. That didn't keep him from examining carefully both the photographs and the details on the restricted-area badges they produced for him. Lance didn't blame him in the slightest. They both knew the powers-that-be were entirely capable of trying to slip someone through with a badge bearing a picture of a chimpanzee, just to see if security were on its toes. Finally the man stepped back, pushed the barricade—which rose easily, being counterweighted—waved them through, and saluted.

Lance returned the salute. "Thank you, sergeant. See you in twenty-four hours!"

"Yes, sir!"

Lance drove on slowly, watching for potholes, wincing slightly as stones hit the underside of his precious car with clinks...

The road divided. Right fork, as he recalled. He took it.

Clink. Clink. Clink.

"You okay?" David said.

"I'm fine. We'll be there in a minute."

He continued negotiating rocks and potholes.

Clink. Clink. Clink.

It hadn't seemed nearly as far last time, when Turso was driving his Ford Explorer with its thirteen-inch clearance.

Clink. Clink. Clink.

THIRTEEN

*Sherwood Road, near Exeter, and a few miles
from R.A.F. Harlsden. 2.10 p.m.*

Superintendent James Hanlon of the Devon and Cornwall
police, notepad and pen in hand, was standing in his
own driveway in his own garden in front of his own house.
Even so, he felt displaced and disconcerted. Sweaty, too, for
though there'd been a lot of rain and the sky was overcast,
there was thunder in the air and the temperature was higher
than it looked — unusually high for the time of year. Someone
on the radio that morning said it was the third warmest April
since 1914.

The door of the black chauffeur-driven 1930s Rolls Royce limousine in front of him had just closed in his face with a soft click.
He was a schoolboy again, abruptly dismissed from the presence of the headmaster. Or perhaps it was worse. Reflections on
the glass prevented him seeing inside the Rolls. So perhaps the
man he'd been talking to had simply disappeared?

Ridiculous. Why should he even imagine such a thing?

Still, there was definitely something about the man... something that made you imagine odd things, things you didn't like
to think about.

Slowly at first, the Rolls started to move. The engine made

no sound that Hanlon could hear. There was only the crunch of tires on gravel. Massive and gleaming, the huge black car rolled away from him, stopped for a moment in the gateway, then pulled forward onto the road, turning left as it did so in the direction of Exeter, finally to disappear along the hedgerow.

Silence, broken only by the chirp of a bird. His wife Alison would know what kind of bird it was. She always did.

He shook his head.

The man in the Rolls had come, so it seemed, to give him instructions. From the moment of the car's appearance in the drive he had been in no doubt as to whose instructions they were. He had once or twice received such instructions before, but always by telephone. On this occasion, however, and for some reason that was not clear to him, they were being given in person.

When he approached, the limousine's window had been lowered. He recognized the occupant at once. He remembered the eyes, and he remembered a conversation at a pub in Hendon when he was still a trainee—a conversation that had changed his life. All that had been quite some years ago. He was aware since then of changes in himself: touches of gray in his hair, for one thing. But the face and the eyes before him appeared not to have changed at all.

"Oh," he said, "it's you! I—oh!" He stopped as a hand with thin fingers and long nails reached out, took his hand, pulled it through the open window, and *sniffed* at it, long and carefully. The grip was hard, cold. Only after two or three minutes was he released. For several moments longer the man in the Rolls did not look at him at all, just sat staring forward. Then at last he turned and looked up through the open window into Hanlon's eyes.

"It seems that you are still with us, Superintendent Hanlon. Still with the academy. Good. Remember your loyalty. And now go and fetch something you can write with."

So he'd fetched notebook and pen and written down his

instructions. He would soon receive a letter. It would be delivered by hand to him in his office at the Heavitree police station. No less a person than the chairman of the academy himself would bring it. And it would give him details as to the arrival of certain unique and valuable pieces of equipment, and what he was to do with them.

The man made him write it all down and then read it back. He felt humiliated and angry.

When he finished, his visitor nodded.

"What you will be asked to do is not difficult," he said, "but it will require precision. You must do it with care. And if you do it successfully, it will cement your relationship with us. Do you understand? Think what you have already received. Who knows what may come in the future?"

Hanlon believed he understood very well. Quite how the "us" to whom the man referred—the "us" he'd met in that pub all those years ago, the "us" that was somehow also "the academy"—had brought about his promotion to the rank of superintendent in the Devon and Cornwall police he wasn't sure, but he had no doubt that it had. And now he was being given a chance to prove his loyalty. And then, as the man said, who knew what else might come? Perhaps (he allowed himself for just a moment to dwell on the thought) perhaps chief constable of the counties of Devon and Cornwall? And with it the chance, at least in one part of England, to put into reality his vision, the vision he'd always had, the vision of a properly organized and disciplined police force upholding the law without fear or favor or tolerance of the slightest infringement in an orderly society. "Isn't that what we all want? It's certainly what the academy wants. Order. Discipline. That means some people controlling the rest—for everyone's benefit, of course. And we see you as a man to help bring it about." That's what the man had said to him in the pub, all those years ago.

And *that*, as he reminded himself from time to time, was what it was all really about. He'd loathed it just now when the fellow seized his hand and dragged it into the car and he'd felt his breath on it and the cold touch of his skin. It had felt like an invasion.

Almost he'd resisted. Almost he'd said, "That's enough!"

But he hadn't.

He'd put up with it.

For a purpose.

He ran a finger around his shirt collar, easing it away from his neck. For a few moments longer he continued to stare after the Rolls.

Then, slowly, he turned and started walking back up the driveway toward the house.

Alison met him by the front door. She was carrying gardening gloves and tools. She turned and looked at him.

"It was nothing," he said in answer to her unspoken question. "Just a man who wanted to talk."

He walked past her into the house. Alison raised an eyebrow and stood still for a moment, then walked down to the flowerbeds and began to trim roses. She worked quickly and skillfully, though her thoughts were elsewhere. Once she made a wrong cut, pruning below the fork instead of above, and shook her head. But she was not overly concerned about the rose.

She could always tell when James was lying.

And this time it was easier than usual.

After all, who goes to fetch pen and paper, then stands and takes notes from a casual passerby who just wants to talk?

FOURTEEN

London, Bayswater. The same afternoon.

The train was on time and the tube was quick, and it was just on a quarter past two when Cecilia arrived at the headquarters of the Academy for Philosophical Studies, one of a row of fine nineteenth-century town houses in an avenue off the Bayswater Road.

Her visit went almost exactly as she expected. When she identified herself at the reception desk she was greeted courteously, at once shown into an office, and within minutes found herself interviewing a bespectacled young administrator who introduced himself as Tom Weaver and was, she suspected, as innocent of the murder of John Stewart Cox as she was herself.

He made no objection to her recording the interview.

"How long have you been working here, Mr. Weaver?" she asked.

"A couple of months, Detective Inspector. I'm just doing it as a temp until I start university."

The young man made no attempt to shield his computer screen as he swung around in his desk chair and checked the academy's records, although he could have turned it away from her field of vision with the slightest push.

John Stewart Cox, it appeared, had been a member of the

academy for a single quarter—the minimum period allowed. But then he'd cancelled his membership.

Weaver chuckled.

Cecilia raised an eyebrow.

He grinned and pointed. "You can see what he said."

She leaned forward and peered. Whoever typed up the record had inserted a comment—presumably Cox's—in the *member's feedback* box. "The lectures were basically codswallop."

Cecilia found herself already liking this John Stewart Cox, just as she liked his sister. Which made the murder all the more heartbreaking.

"And you," she said, "do you think the lectures are codswallop, Mr. Weaver?"

"I've never been to any," he said. "They're generally in the evening and I just work here in the office during the day. I'm going to read art history at university and art's what I'm interested in and I gather the people here think that's a waste of space."

Of course they would.

"And you've no indication of any further contact between Mr. Cox and the academy?"

"Nothing here. And what's here's all I know."

She believed him.

And that was that. All perfectly reasonable. There was no more reason to connect the academy with the murder of John Stewart Cox than there was to connect any of the dozen or so other institutions whose cards had been in the little pile on his desk.

No reason at all—save the fact that this was yet one more occasion when the academy had appeared on the fringe of an untimely death. And that *was* a reason, even though you couldn't bring them into court for it.

So now, at a quarter to three in the afternoon, Cecilia stood in the Bayswater Road, opposite the park, and reflected that she was free to do anything she liked.

She smiled, took out her mobile, went to her contacts, and called Saint Andrew's Rectory.

She got Jim, Michael's secretary.

"He's at Bishop's House at a meeting," he said, "but I know he'll want to see you. He's due back at four and so far as I can see he hasn't got anything else until there's a meeting here at six. Do you want to come for a cup of tea?"

"I'd love to come for a cup of tea," she said.

FIFTEEN

L ance sighed and eased his foot off the accelerator.
     At last they'd arrived.

Trees had been cleared to create a fenced area about the size of a soccer field. Inside was a single-story building, cream painted. There were overhead lights and a couple of parked vehicles. There was an additional hut, with flies buzzing around something on the roof.

"You know," David said, "this place could pass for a parking lot."

"I guess it could," Lance said. "But with a little more firepower."

With a good deal more firepower, as they both knew. This was Alpha-2, a control center for the MX missile—a weapon system so deadly that its Pentagon progenitors had referred to it almost from the beginning as the Peacekeeper. Built when the cold war between East and West had seemed as inevitable as breathing, the system remained decades later, aging but still armed, a continuing monument to unease.

Naturally its missiles were no longer directed at Moscow. Now, who knew where they might be pointed next? Téhéran? Pyongyang? Beijing? Anything was possible, and of course

David was right. It wasn't just that the control centers looked like parking lots. As far as Lance was concerned, they were by now so familiar they were starting to *feel* like parking lots.

"The trouble with missile silos," David went on, "is they're all alike. You've seen one, you've seen them all."

"So what do you suggest? Artwork? Fountains?"

"I'll have to think about it."

At the entrance to the compound yet another security police-man checked their identification as if he'd never seen them before, this one not only examining their documents but also walking all the way around the MG, peering under it, and staring inside at the space behind their seats. Good thing they weren't carrying a bomb. Finally he stepped back, saluted, and told them where to park.

Lance slid the MG into the indicated space and switched off. He got out and stretched, smiling as David, who was taller than he, unwound himself from the passenger seat and blinked in the sunlight.

Already the inevitable R.A.F. security policeman was at hand—this time one they really had *not* seen before, who watched unsmiling while they took small handgrips from the car. Still unsmiling he checked the contents. Lance's irritation mounted as he gazed long and suspiciously—or was it lecher-ously?—at the photograph of Sophie.

"Thank you, sergeant," he said when he got the grip back. "Are you sure there's nothing else you'd like to check?"

"Not at the moment, sir."

Sarcasm clearly did not register.

The security man led them to the cream-colored building and punched in a code, ostentatiously turning his body so they'd have no chance to read what he entered. Lance exchanged a look with David, who rolled his eyes. In a sense, to be sure, the man was right, but they'd have looked away in any case. That was part of the etiquette of a system built entirely on two prin-ciples: "need to know" and "never alone." They would never need to know the codes for entry to the control center since they would never enter it unaccompanied, and what they didn't need to know they mustn't know.

The double doors slid back grinding and squeaking (they had squeaked last time) to expose the elevator, cavernous and dim. The drop in temperature as they entered it was abrupt, and Lance shivered, then blinked as the doors closed again, still grinding, abruptly cutting them off from sky, trees, and the security man.

His stomach lurched. They were descending.

A jerky stop.

The doors slid back, squeaky as ever, and though by now he was expecting it, the shrill sound set his teeth on edge.

"Typical," David muttered. "Billions of dollars' worth of technology, and nobody spared a buck for a can of oil."

They stepped into the corridor, more dimly lit than he remembered from their last visit. Institutional green. Maybe it was just as well it was dimly lit.

Facing them at the other end of the corridor was the door. Thirteen tons of it, nuclear-blast-proof.

"Okay," he said, glancing at David. "Let's go."

They walked slowly, the only sound their own footfalls and the hum of air conditioning.

Footfalls… *echo in the memory / Down the passage which we did not take / Towards the door we never opened…*

"Into the rose garden."

"What?"

He had spoken that last line aloud.

"T. S. Eliot," he said. "*Four Quartets.* My grandfather used to quote it all the time."

David grinned. "I was pretty sure it wasn't the *U.C.M.J.*"

The door was opening. Lance felt himself grow tense. He always did, just for a moment, when one of those doors started to open at the end of a corridor.

"A corridor and a door," David said, this time reading him

rather well. "Possibly symbolizing an unknown threat. Or an opportunity. Or both. Psychology 101."

"Touché!"

There in the doorway was Gianni Turso, the captain who had taken them around on their orientation.

"Lance, David—hi! Good to see you both. Welcome again to Alfa-2."

SIXTEEN

Saint Andrew's Rectory. 4.15 the same afternoon.

The meeting at Bishop's House had gone on longer than Michael Aarons expected, and it had been acrimonious. Surely there was nothing more depressing than ecclesial and clerical acrimony, gilded as it invariably was with self-righteousness, and surely he himself was as bad as any. Always needing everyone to understand what a good chap he was, kind to children and small animals…

He shook his head and glanced at his watch. He had nothing until the finance committee at six, and at least that was in the vicarage, so he didn't have to go anywhere. He was tired and more than ready for a break.

He was barely through the front door when Jim emerged from the office.

"You've got a visitor, Father. I put her in your study."

Michael's heart sank. Another meeting was the last thing he needed.

"Hello, Michael."

Cecilia Cavaliere was standing at the top of the stairs, sunlight from an upper window gleaming on her hair.

Now that Michael came to think about it he wasn't tired at all and another meeting was *exactly* what he needed.

"I'll bring you both a fresh pot of tea and some more of Mrs. Evans's biscuits, shall I?"

"Thanks, Jim. That would be perfect."

Jim stood and watched as Father Michael went up the stairs and his visitor kissed him in her Italian fashion on each cheek.

"Cecilia, I'm so glad you're here, I've been wanting to talk to you about *Sanditon* — I'm ashamed it took me so long to get round to it. But I have at last and it's marvelous. Thanks so much for telling me about it!"

"Oh you read it, did you? Isn't it wonderful…"

They disappeared into his study.

Jim smiled. In his opinion Father Michael worked much too hard, never took enough time off, and didn't have any fun at all. And him still quite a young man! So it was good to see him for once looking as if he were enjoying himself. And she was certainly a beautiful young woman. And smart, too, from all he'd heard. A detective inspector! You don't get to be that at her age unless you're pretty special.

He went to the kitchen and put the kettle on. Then, after a moment's consideration, he took out some decent china.

Jim took Cecilia to Paddington Station in Michael's car, and she caught the 6.30 to Exeter. It was slower than the 6.03 but much less crowded, and she was happy to sit in a corner seat in an otherwise empty second-class carriage and reflect.

Michael had been as baffled about the latest emergence of the academy into their lives as she was. He conceded, as she did, that this time there really might not be a connection, but he also conceded, as she did, that there might.

This could be just a robbery that had gone wrong.

Or that could be what they were supposed think.

What we can't show, we don't know.

Still, she was happy she'd kept Michael in the loop. The sick feeling she'd had when she first heard about the academy's connection to John Stewart Cox had gone.

Michael had seemed pleased to see her, even though he looked rather tired.

And she'd enjoyed her tea with him.

So it wasn't all bad, was it?

In fact, now she came to think about it, it hadn't at all been a bad day off.

Considering she hadn't actually *had* much of it off.

SEVENTEEN

London, later that day.

The days that followed his conversation in the bar were busy for George Jameson, who did not see his drinking companion again. He might have forgotten completely about their meeting had it not been for an unpleasant dream the night following it.

He was with his old friend from the grammar school, George Charles Humphrey Blair—"Blairsie," they'd called him. A bit of a drip he'd been, really, but back then he seemed to admire George and so George had put up with him. Of course they'd lost touch when they left school and George hadn't thought about him for years. Someone a few years' ago told him he thought Blairsie had married a nurse and they'd gone off to be missionaries in South Africa or somewhere, which would be the sort of daft thing old Blairsie *would* do. But he didn't know if it was true.

Anyway, in his dream Blairsie and he were the thirteen-year-old schoolboys they'd been back then. There was a picnic set out on the grass—beautiful sandwiches and cool lemonade—and the man who'd talked with him in the bar was there in blazer and cricket flannels and a school cap, offering them bowls of strawberries and cream. Blairsie was shouting out—"Don't touch it, Jameson! Don't touch it!" But George was hungry and the strawberries looked delicious so he took them anyway, and as he held them in his hand they turned into the most revolting maggots and the man from the bar was laughing and Blairsie was still shouting and he woke up.

It was just a dream, of course, but he found it curiously disconcerting. And it stayed with him for days.

Odd, what tricks the mind will play.

EIGHTEEN

Exeter Cathedral. Tuesday, 5th May. 10.00 a.m.

The funeral and requiem were in the cathedral on the morning of the day following the coroner's inquest. When Cecilia arrived she saw Verity Jones in the back row, elegant in black, and went and sat next to her. It was Cecilia's habit to attend the funerals of victims in cases that involved her — as a sign of respect and because you never knew what interesting and perhaps revealing behavior you might see among those who came to mourn.

On the present occasion, however, she found herself far more emotionally involved than she'd expected or was usual for her. It was partly, of course, the cathedral. She loved the cathedral — the gothic arches, the windows, the images. It was a pity religion had such an awful history, all those persecutions and burning people at stakes. And a lot of the people she knew thought religion was just nonsense anyway. Yet somehow, despite all that, when she was in a place like this, she'd like to have been part of it.

She sighed.

After readings from the Bible, various people, including his sister, spoke about John Stewart Cox. Even allowing for such degrees of kindness in recollection as are natural on such occasions, it was obvious that he'd been an affectionate, talented young man, with a wicked sense of humor. His sister's and a couple of his students' reminiscences hovered between laughter and tears.

After those tributes, an actor friend of the family read Dylan Thomas's "Do not go gentle into that good night."

> *Do not go gentle into that good night.*
>
> *Rage, rage against the dying of the light...*

Apparently, it was a poem that John Cox admired. Cecilia thought it appropriate. She was also glad they hadn't picked a piece many people these days seemed to want at funerals. "Death is nothing at all. It does not count. I have only slipped away into the next room." When that was read she always found herself wanting to shout out, "That's a damned lie! You *haven't* just slipped into the next room. If you had, we could come and hug you."

Michael told her once that Saint Paul called death "the last enemy." Now that was more like it. There was a man who called a spade a spade.

The dean summed up the readings, the tributes, and the poetry by speaking about the resurrection of Jesus Christ and Christian hope.

"Even," he said, "when we're not faced with tragedies such as the one that appalls us today in the taking from us of John Stewart, in the loss of this beautiful young life, still we know that we all, sooner or later, stand on the brink and precipice of death. And then what awaits us? A positive and hopeful response to that question, and the promise that we, and not only we but the entire created order, shall share in its unfolding: these are a consequence — not the only consequence but *a* consequence — of our belief that God raised Jesus Christ from the dead. The life of faith and grace is to live in hope of this — let us be frank — for most of us, most of the time, unimaginable redemption, and to live as those who are actively preparing for it. Our every attempt to promote justice, compassion, and graceful order is a participation in that preparation and hence, however apparently useless or defeated, *never* in vain."

At the offertory, the British Concert played the musette movement from Handel's Concerto Grosso number six, and again Mary Cox played the solo. The bulletin said it was one of John Stewart Cox's favorite pieces. Cecilia was sure Ms. Cox played it well but also realized she was in no condition to judge, for the beauty of it was breaking her heart.

When it came to communion she wasn't sure what to do. She wanted to receive, and she knew that Anglican altars were open to non-Anglicans, but she was, after all, "the police." Perhaps right now it wasn't appropriate?

But then little Miss Perfect who'd grown up Church in Wales and who (of course!) always knew exactly what was proper in church as in every other situation bent down and took her hand. Their usual roles were somehow reversed and seconds later Cecilia found herself lined up in the aisle with everyone else, and minutes after that she was at the altar rail, with Verity — sweet, funny Verity — kneeling beside her. And it was the right place to be.

"The body of Christ."

"The blood of Christ."

"Amen," she said, and crossed herself, as Verity did.

Back in her seat with Verity beside her, she glanced around, conscious of soaring gothic and sounding organ all about her and the choir singing.

> *The Lord shall preserve thee from all evil;*
>
> *Yea, it is even he that shall keep thy soul.*

Yes, well, that's all very well but is it true? I mean, you didn't manage to preserve John Stewart Cox from all evil, did you? If you had, we wouldn't be here.

The choir persisted.

The Lord shall preserve thy going out, and thy coming in,

From this time forth for evermore.

Cecilia shook her head, but the voices were unrelenting:

Requiem aeternam dona eis, et lux perpetua —

Lux perpetua!

Suddenly she saw.

The arches and pillars of the cathedral were throbbing with light, *lux perpetua* — billions and billions of molecules in everlasting and glorious dance, and she a part of it.

And she heard.

She heard the music of the dance, music beyond all the music she'd ever heard, at once its source and its sustainer. She tingled with delight.

And she knew.

She knew that John Stewart Cox *was* well, and that all those people over the ages who'd been persecuted and burnt at stakes were also well, and that all the things that concerned her would be well so that finally —

It was over. Her moment of vision, ecstasy, delirium, whatever it was, ended as suddenly as it began.

— luceat eis.

The choir completed the phrase. It seemed she had missed nothing. Then their voices soared and repeated it, again and again:

Et lux perpetua,

perpetua,

luceat,

luceat,

luceat eis.

It was only an echo of that other music, but it *was* an echo, and therefore glorious.

Quite what had just happened to her she wasn't sure. But she was sure that it was beautiful, almost more beautiful than she could bear. And that it had somehow swept up into its beauty all the pain and sorrow that surrounded her, and made them precious.

Though it was over, the memory of it was still with her, filling her with a sweet, wonderful longing.

She sighed, then buried her head in her hands.

When the service ended she intended to slip quietly away, but before she could do that Mary Cox came up to her and took her hand.

"Thank you for coming to John's funeral," she said.

Cecilia smiled and nodded and held Mary Cox's hand, but at that moment she couldn't think of anything to say.

Actually, she didn't think she could have said it if she *had* thought of anything.

She seemed to have lost her voice.

Fortunately, it didn't seem to matter.

Verity Jones fell in beside her as she walked across the cathedral lawn toward the cars.

"Are you all right, ma'am?"

Dear Verity, she felt like hugging her.

She contented herself by smiling and saying, "I'm okay, Verity. But thanks for asking."

At least her voice had come back.

Perhaps in time she would want to talk about what had happened to her in the cathedral. But not yet. For now, she just wanted to hold onto it — whatever it was.

And there was another thing.

Quite how it followed from what had just happened she wasn't sure, but apparently it did: she was now more determined than ever to do whatever she could to find and bring to justice whoever was responsible for the murder of John Stewart Cox.

Costi quel costi, she said softly to herself.

Whatever it took.

NINETEEN

London. Gordon and Settler's, Merchant Bankers.
Wednesday, May 6th. 7.45 a.m.

The telephone on George Jameson's desk was ringing. Not one of the main office phones—this was his personal line. He looked at his watch. Odd that there should be a call for him at this hour. He'd only just arrived, and he was early.

He picked up.

"Jameson here."

"Have you seen the news?" It was Bob Hodgson, his friend in overseas acquisitions. He sounded excited.

"What news?"

"Look at *The Times*, man. Front page. Third column, halfway down. I think you'll be interested."

"All right, then. I will."

George replaced the handset and reached for his briefcase, which contained this morning's *Times* still unopened.

He glanced at the relevant column.

Good God almighty!

Ruggles's BMW had gone out of control on the M4 and collided with a petrol tanker. There had been a massive explosion which neither driver survived. The driver of the tanker left a widow and three young children. Ruggles was unmarried.

The hair on the back of George's head prickled. There was no mention in the news story of the police suspecting foul play. Ruggles appeared to have fallen asleep at the wheel.

So perhaps the conversation at the bar was merely a coincidence?

Or perhaps not.

At any rate, it really did seem that nothing now stood between George and his partnership. That, evidently, was the opinion of Bob Hodgson, and Bob Hodgson was generally reckoned to know a thing or two about such matters.

TWENTY

Heavitree Road Police Station. The same day. 9.00 a.m.

"I called this briefing," Cecilia said, "because I think it's time to see where we are on everything that's come in."

Facing her were DS Verity Jones, dramatic today in scarlet and black, the officers and the two SOCOs who'd been at the crime-scene on the first day, and, in his wheelchair, Joseph Stirrup their computer genius. He was there not only because Cecilia was convinced there was nothing it was possible to do with a computer that Joseph couldn't do, but also because she found his insights generally valuable.

First, she described briefly the interviews she and DS Jones had conducted with Mary Cox and her family.

"Now, let's look at where we are with the physical evidence. Doctor Foss, I think you're going to tell us what you've learned from the dust."

Cecilia took her seat as Foss advanced to his section of the whiteboard. He went quickly through the evidence from Mary's shoes, which supported her version of what had happened. Then he continued, "Now, here's the interesting bit. We found other shoe prints in the sitting room and in the bedroom that didn't fit with anyone we know, including a right and left together by the bed where the victim lay, near where the scissors were found. They were size twelve."

A dramatic pause.

"Made by a pair of Danner Desert Acadia military boots," he said. "No special distinguishing marks, unfortunately, but they're pretty spectacular boots anyway."

"So," Cecilia said, "we're looking for someone with large feet and a taste for American bother boots."

"Expensive bother boots," he said. "You couldn't expect to pick these up for much under a hundred and fifty quid."

"Are we checking suppliers?" She looked at Verity, who said nobody in Exeter had sold a pair like them.

"But of course someone could have bought them on line, ma'am."

She turned to Joseph.

"Among some people they're a bit of a fashion item," he said, "and there are quite a lot of online sites where the murderer could have got them. I'm checking them all, but as I said, there's a lot of them and it's taking time."

Shoe prints weren't the best kind of evidence but could certainly add something if they ever had anything else to go on.

"Well, keep at it, Joseph. If you get a hit there it could be important."

They went on to fingerprints, which weren't helpful, and then to blood, which was.

"Most of the blood spilled in the apartment was the victim's," Dr. Foss said. "But there was also someone else's blood, a few drops on the carpet and some in the washbasin in the bathroom, and traces in the u-pipe under the sink—as you thought, Detective Inspector. Whoever it was seems to have received a cut, maybe in a fight, and then maybe tried to wash it. That means we might have a DNA sample from the killer. We've run a check with the usual databases but so far no matches."

He looked at Gibbings, who said, "And that includes the international databases. No luck there either."

Serial numbers and descriptions of the TV and the laptop had been circulated not only locally but far afield. No leads had emerged from interviews with the victim's known contacts — including the Academy for Philosophical Studies — on which Cecilia reported. She noted that the academy had appeared on the fringes of unlawful killings they'd investigated on another occasion, but — as Verity pointed out — those killings all seemed to revolve around one man connected to the academy, a man who'd subsequently committed suicide while in police custody. So perhaps the academy as an institution was not involved.

"Nonetheless," Cecilia added, "if the name of the Academy for Philosophical Studies *does* crop up again in connection with *anything* else that *any* of you are doing in regards to this case, then however bizarre or faint the connection, I want to know about it."

She looked around at the group.

"To sum up, then: the physical evidence so far supports Mary Cox's account. It also suggests there was an intruder, and we're regarding that person as the likely killer. We haven't as yet identified a suspect. Following a lead such as the boots might get us to one.

"Now, before we adjourn can anyone think of anything we aren't doing that we could be doing? Any other ideas? Anything else we need to notice? Even if you think it's daft, try me."

They all shook their heads.

Twenty-One

London. Thursday 7th May.

Whatever scruples the board members of Gordon and Settler's may have had earlier regarding George Jameson and his appointment to a partnership, they moved swiftly following Ruggles's death, which was on Tuesday, May 5th. They met on the Thursday immediately following, and Jameson was appointed to the vacant partnership without opposition.

On the day following his appointment, a letter arrived at George's apartment inviting him to accept an honorary fellowship offered by the Academy for Philosophical Studies and suggesting he might care to make a donation to the academy of fifty thousand pounds.

Well he had, after all, got what he wanted.

It wasn't as if he couldn't afford the money.

And if the academy had indeed had something to do with Ruggles's death, then he was not so foolish as to imagine that what had happened to Ruggles couldn't happen to him — even though he told himself it was quite possible that Ruggles had simply fallen asleep at the wheel.

Or not.

He went to his computer, added the academy to his list of payees, and sent the donation at once.

Evidently there were staff at the academy who worked weekends and worked fast, for on the morning following his payment of the fifty thousand pounds George received an email from them in which he was thanked for his donation and invited to a cocktail party that same evening at their headquarters in Bayswater.

Of course he immediately emailed back his acceptance.

TWENTY-TWO

London, a day later.

"Cecilia, I think I've got something for you."

Following her account of John Cox's comments about the academy's lectures, Michael had followed a hunch of his own. Dennis O'Flaherty was a gregarious, amusing fellow who worked in a wine bar near Bayswater and could talk his way in and out of anywhere. Michael had asked him for help a couple of times previously when he'd needed information.

"I deliberately didn't mention Cox's *name* to Dennis," he told Cecilia, "because I didn't want people remembering what they might think someone *wanted* them to remember. So I just asked him to see if anyone recalled any rows with students in recent weeks. Well, friend Dennis chatted up some of the people who work in the kitchens, and some of them laughed and told him about Johnny Cox. Apparently he was a bit of a lad and flirted with the waitresses and they liked him. Anyway, he came out from one of the academy lectures one evening when the hall was full of people and said, 'Who runs this place? Where's his office?' As it happened the chairman was actually standing there, talking to some important people, so Cox goes straight up to him and says, "Do you know what's being handed out in those lectures you're running? I've been to two now. They were supposed to be on the basics of philosophy, but they were utter codswallop."

Michael paused.

"They actually heard him use that word?"

"They actually heard him use that word. At least, that's what Dennis says and I *know* I hadn't said the word to him. Again, I was particularly careful not to. Cox went on to say something like, 'If your chap thinks all our thinking is just atoms moving round in our brains, what reason's he got to think he's right? He's refuted himself!' The chairman said something about Cox being young and ignorant and having a lot to learn, and Cox said, 'No doubt I do have a lot to learn—but not here! I came because I understood this place had something to do with study and something to do with philosophy. It doesn't seem to have much to do with either, so I'm going. Goodbye.' The chairman was furious over being harangued in front of all those people and of course the staff was highly amused, which is no doubt why they remembered it."

"I suppose we can't talk to these kitchen staff?"

"Cecilia, they're foreigners, working here illegally—Immigration could have them deported in the blink of an eye. Dennis wouldn't even tell *me* who they were, and of course under the circumstances I couldn't press him. He was doing me a favor."

"I hear you."

"But I think the story's likely to be true, all the same. They came up with the right name *and* the right word."

"A perfect example—if you want to know what's going on, ask the people in the kitchen. Oh, Michael, thank you so much! Obviously these people would never have talked to me, or anyone like me. I really appreciate this!"

"Oh, Cecilia, you are most welcome!"

***

Later that day Cecilia fixed a note to the case whiteboard.

"I have a report that I think likely to be true, though it cannot be confirmed or attributed, that John Cox publicly offended the chairman of the Academy for Philosophical Studies in London last June. I continue to be interested in any other appearance of the academy in this investigation, even if it's only on the fringes."

TWENTY-THREE

Saint Andrew's Vicarage. That evening.

Michael was at his desk.

He gazed at the silver-framed black and white photograph of his parents, who gazed back at him.

He sighed.

He'd finished preparing his sermon for tomorrow, the fifth Sunday of Easter. He'd enjoyed doing that, but now he knew he really ought to turn his attention to a set of diocesan finance sheets. They'd been sitting beside the computer since Wednesday, and he was sure he would not enjoy them at all.

The telephone rang. He picked the handset up with a smile, happy for the interruption.

He was even happier when the interruption turned out to be Cecilia Cavaliere.

"How do you think your murder investigation is going overall?" he said after they'd chatted for a few minutes.

"I'd say it's in a kind of limbo." Cecilia sighed. "We've got various things we're following up. We've got various odd connections—like the academy, which despite suggestive things we've found out—some of them thanks to you—still may not have anything to do with the case. We have leads, notably a pair of boots. What we don't have is a suspect. Obviously we're going to keep looking, but it may be we won't get further until we have some kind of break, say, one of the leads we're working on produces something. Or somebody or something quite unexpected turns up. I've never done any fishing, but I've watched them fishing on the River Exe, and sometimes I think trying to solve a crime is a bit like that. You set everything up. You do everything you can with what you've got. But then you've just got to be patient and sit and wait till you get a bite."

"So you preside over a sort of organized chaos?"

She laughed. "There's nothing organized about it!"

They talked for a few minutes longer, until Michael began to feel that the conversation was drawing to a close.

"Michael, do you have another minute?"

"Of course!"

"Actually, I think I mean do you have several minutes?"

"I think I have quite a lot of minutes." He looked down at his desk. "Stuff the diocesan finances," he said, more or less to himself.

"What?"

"Oh… just babbling. What do you have to fill up several minutes?"

"It's just that I want to ask you about something. You know that night at Cranston College, when Charlie Brown died?"

"I doubt that I'll ever forget it."

"Me too. But I'd like to know what you think about what we saw. I mean, what actually *was* it? Was it real?"

"Oh."

"Michael, I'm sorry for springing this on you. It's just that now something *else* has happened, and I'd like to know what you think about what we saw."

Michael was quiet for a minute. Cecilia waited.

"I suppose the first thing to say is that it all depends on what you mean by real," he said. "I mean, that night we had what I suppose most people would call a religious experience. Obviously that experience — what we saw — wasn't part of our everyday reality. But is that the only kind of reality there is? If you think it is, then obviously what we saw was an illusion. But if you *don't* think that—and as it happens, I don't—then of course what we saw may have been real but involving reality of another order from the everyday."

"Well the thing is, I think I saw it again. Not quite the same—but, well, I saw it. Glimpsed that other reality."

He listened intently as she told him, stumbling a little, about an experience she'd had in the cathedral.

"It was wonderful," she said, "glorious, the way it was glorious in the tunnel—but only for a few seconds. Then it was gone. But if it was real and not just my imagination, why me? Why us? Why doesn't everyone have experiences like that?"

He considered carefully before answering.

"I *think*," he said finally, "that in fact a great many people have experiences like yours. There's been a lot of research done over the last few decades, and one of the things that seems to emerge consistently from it is that lots of people, when they think about it, are aware of having had *something* they can identify as a religious experience, the sense of an overwhelming, gracious presence—the sort of thing you describe. These people aren't believers, necessarily—indeed, they may be agnostics or atheists—but still they admit to the experience. Of course if they're atheists they don't see it as pointing to anything real. For them it's just a momentary delusion, a trick of the mind, and of course it *can* be explained psychologically in all sorts of ways. But still they admit to having it."

"Are they a type? Poets and madmen?"

"Actually they're not. Hippolyta was much nearer the mark. As I understand the research, the more intelligent and better educated someone is, the more likely they are to have such an experience. A friend of mine had one when she was a teenager. It came to her as she was looking into a flower. She says it changed her life. And I've just been reading a book by Arnold Benz, the Swiss astrophysicist. He talks about an experience he had in New Mexico. He and his colleagues had spent a frustrating day trying to receive radio waves from outer space. Then he went for a walk. And as he was walking, he had this experience, this sense of *union* with the cosmos, of reconciliation, of grace. After that, he was more determined than ever to go on with his scientific work. Which he has done, to this day. That was how it affected *him*."

A long silence.

"Are you still there?"

"Sorry! I was thinking. Michael, the most extraordinary thing about it was that just for a moment I *knew*. That John Cox was all right. That everything was going to be all right. Or I thought I knew. But I couldn't know, could I? What we can't show we don't know. Or do we?"

"I think that science and faith both lead to knowledge, but not the same *kinds* of knowledge and not in the same way. For scientific knowledge, you have to analyze—keep yourself out of it as much as possible—be as objective as you can, and anybody else has to be able to arrive at the same answer as you if they take the same steps. As you say, what we can't show we don't know. And of course what we *can* show through such knowledge is often interesting and important. And if you don't mind my saying so, in work like yours where you're trying to determine who committed a crime and not arrest the wrong person, it's crucial."

He stopped, suddenly uncertain whether she was still with him.

"Keep talking," she said, seeming to read his uncertainty. "I think I see where you're going."

"Well, okay. Where I'm going is, I think the kind of knowledge we get through faith is different because by definition we *can't* keep ourselves out of it. Faith *means* being committed, involved, taking a chance. Which means, of course, that we can also always back away from it.

"You can say about what happened to you in the cathedral,

oh, I was just overtired, or a bit emotional, or heard some music, or got something in my eye and it made me go all teary, or whatever — and maybe you were, or did. And to dismiss it like that sounds terribly scientific and up-to-date, doesn't it? But — and this is something I got from Benz's book — to insist that that's *all* there was to your religious experience is actually no more a *scientific* decision than to decide God spoke to you through it. *Neither* decision is demonstrable scientifically. But if we *do* decide to go along with the experience, to say 'Yes!' to it, — then the experience of millions of people over centuries has been that they've come to new knowledge — a different kind of knowledge from scientific knowledge, but still knowledge."

"It will be more like when we trust a friend. Or love someone. And get to *know* them."

"Exactly. And if the experience of all these people is right — indeed, if my *own* experience is right — then it seems to me that God's a modest friend who'll hang about for ages waiting for us. But as with any other friend, until we choose, until we say 'Yes, I'll take a chance on you,' of course we don't get to know what they're really like."

They were both quiet for a moment.

"And by the way," he said, "that thing you thought you knew — that everything was going to be all right, no matter how bad things look? Well, again, other people have had that exact same experience. Julian of Norwich, for one. She had a vision in which she was told, 'All shall be well and all manner of thing shall be well.' As it happens she was a feisty lady and she argued about it, even in her vision! She said something like, 'Everything's such a mess, Lord, that with all due respect I just don't see how it can possibly all be well,' and the answer she got was, 'What's impossible for you isn't impossible for me.' She wrote her visions down — *Revelations of Divine Love*, she called them. I could lend them to you, if you like. I could lend you Benz's book too."

"Thank you. I'd like that."

"I'm sorry, I'm really not an expert." He sighed. "I think maybe I should put you in touch with a real spiritual director to talk about your questions, someone who'd be better at—"

But Cecilia was laughing, a rich mezzo-soprano laugh that came over the phone and took his breath away.

"Oh, Michael, I can see you know *nothing* about the matter and haven't thought about it *at all!*" Her voice grew more serious, though there was still laughter in it. "More precisely, you've only thought about it just enough to be able to give clear, lucid opinions so that a complete nitwit on the subject like me can follow without difficulty. And you do it at the drop of a hat. No warning. No chance to prepare. I think you're brilliant!"

"Oh, well… thank you." He was rather glad she couldn't see him at the moment. He was sure he was blushing.

"Don't mention it," she said. "I knew you'd be brilliant. That's why I asked you. And now Figaro's jumping about, insisting he's much more interesting than my religious experiences and in any case it's time for his walk. So I suppose I'd better go. Goodnight. And dear Michael, thank you."

"Goodnight, Cecilia. It was a great pleasure. And God bless you."

He put the phone down and sat back in his chair.

His pulse was racing.

She'd called him dear. And she'd said she thought he was brilliant.

And he thought she was wonderful… and absolutely stunning.

He let himself daydream for just a moment, then shook his head.

Don't be ridiculous, Michael. She called you as a friend and a priest and you had the privilege of being able to help, at least a little. And she was grateful. And being the honest, open person she is, she said so. But that doesn't mean you should be getting any foolish ideas. As you've told yourself before, a woman like her must have dozens of terrific, *younger* men to choose from. Be grateful for the honor she's given you.

Be a good friend.

He looked at his desk.

Oh, Lord.

The diocesan finances were still waiting.

Ah, but wait a minute.

He ought to go and find Julian's *Revelations* and Benz's *Future of the Universe* before he forgot his promise to send them to Cecilia. Colledge and Walsh's translation of Julian was in the bookshelf in the passage, and Benz was—

Who was he kidding?

As if there were the remotest chance of his forgetting a promise he'd made to Cecilia Cavaliere!

TWENTY-FOUR

London. Monday, May 11ᵗʰ.

George got in earlier than usual from the office, fixed himself a drink, and then turned on the television to see how the New York Stock exchange, which was of course five hours behind, was faring.

But the set was tuned to one of the other channels, and before he had time to change to teletext he found himself staring at images of an extraordinarily beautiful young girl. He stayed his hand. After a few minutes he realized the channel was showing a film of Shakespeare's *Romeo and Juliet*. At first he watched only for the next appearance of the gorgeous girl, but then, despite himself, he was hooked. He sat, entranced, until the end.

> *For never was a story of more woe,*
>
> *Than this of Juliet and her Romeo.*

They'd died for love. Yet surely the prince wasn't entirely right: it was a story of woe, but to love someone so much that one couldn't go on living without them, wasn't that also beautiful? Could one really experience a love so powerful that one would die for it? The girl in the film was a teenager, of course—but in some ways she'd reminded him of Ceci, a very young Ceci.

There were times when he missed Ceci.

Of course he missed her in bed. It wasn't just that she was hot—though she was—and somehow had the gift of being sexy and funny at the same time, so you spent half the time laughing and half the time making love. But it wasn't just that. Ceci had also wanted the kind of love *Romeo and Juliet* was about—a love you were committed to—a love you'd die for. And when it got so that the love was no longer exciting and new, but familiar and homely and more like a comfortable old shoe than a glamorous jewel, she'd still thought you should stick with it.

So was she right?

Suddenly he was filled with yearning for her.

Suppose he went down to Exeter and found her and said he'd been a fool and asked her to take him back?

Well, of course, she'd tell him to get lost. That was what she'd done some months' ago when he'd called her and asked her out for a drink.

Or would she? The fact was, that time when he called her, he'd fancied a night with her but certainly nothing more, and she'd seen straight through his little ploy. But suppose now he said, "I'm sorry. I've been a cheat and a liar and a fool and I've wrecked things. Please forgive me. Please take me back"—and meant it? Suppose he did that?

And even if she did turn him down, wouldn't it still be good if for once he admitted to her *and to himself* that he'd thrown away something richer than anything else in his whole damn life?

And Ceci was generous hearted. So suppose she *didn't* turn him down?

Suppose she took him back.

Well, Ceci being Ceci, it would be forever.

Ceci was like that. That's what she believed in.

Perhaps in time they'd have a kid. Maybe a little boy who

looked like him! And she'd be a wife who was beautiful inside as well as out, who'd be—

Forever!

Abruptly, he went cold.

Was that what he wanted?

Screaming babies?

In-laws?

She'd be putting on weight.

Breasts starting to sag.

Gray hairs.

His yearning for her died as abruptly as it had risen.

All right, so she was good in bed. But then, so were a thousand other beautiful women, and he could afford them all.

What, after all, had happened when he called her that time a few months ago? She'd got on her moral high horse about their break-up and couldn't see he was offering her a good time—offering them *both* a good time—if only she'd had the smarts to take it.

Even back when they were married she'd never really understood anything. One time he'd tried explaining to her how ethics are just tricks our genes play on us so we'll co-operate. "To live *beyond* morality," he'd said, "that's the philosophy of the future."

And what had she done?

She'd laughed.

She'd actually had the gall to *laugh*—and then said she'd like to hear him say all those cool things about morality the next time someone nicked his wallet. As if *that* was anything to do with anything! But that was a woman for you. As a sex, they seemed incapable of logic.

Even Freja, with all her modern ideas, had started clinging after a few months. Finally one night she'd gone all Swedish and serious. "It isn't a matter of *morals*, George. There are *instincts* for commitment between man and woman. Those instincts are basic. We disobey them at our peril."

That was when he decided to send her packing.
He chuckled. Maybe she had those instincts.
He didn't!

Later that evening he met his friend Bob Hodgson for a drink. They were in one of his favorite places—the Victoria, just off Sussex Gardens. After they'd talked a while about their day in the city and the financial situation generally, he changed the subject and mentioned watching Shakespeare's *Romeo and Juliet*, and its odd, though temporary, affect on him.

Bob shook his head. "Poetry can fill your head with all sorts of rubbish. Steer clear of it. I dare say that's why Plato wouldn't have them in the republic—poets, I mean. They cause too much trouble. Words… and the theatre… they're dangerous. Stick to money. And sex."

"I guess so." George nodded. Then he brightened up. "Anyway, the good news is that a sharp dose of reality"—he gestured towards the pub with its chattering customers and then to his drink on the bar beside him—"can work a perfectly efficient cure."

"I'll drink to that," Bob said.

"You know, George," he said a few minutes later, suddenly serious, "I'd be sorry to see you involved in complications with a woman again, and especially with your ex, from all I've heard about her. You'd become half the man you are. Yes, like most of us you need a woman occasionally: but you've found a reliable agency, and the problem's solved. You get a woman when you need one *and* you have some variety. After all, just because you fancy lamb chops for dinner tonight, it doesn't follow you're going to want lamb chops tomorrow, does it? Still less that you're going to want lamb chops every night for the rest of your life!"

The two men laughed.

"I'll drink to that," George said.

And did.

At a shaded table opposite the bar, the consultant, who had been watching and listening to the two men's conversation for some time, nodded with satisfaction. Evidently George was still nicely on track.

For a moment, earlier this afternoon, he'd been worried.

TWENTY-FIVE

Exeter. Tuesday, May 12th.

The murder of John Stewart Cox, a young man of good character living in a respectable and prosperous part of the city of Exeter, though of little interest nationally, was for the generally crime-starved west-country press something of a godsend. His sister's being a distinguished musician made the story even better. So naturally when the story broke they ran something about it every day—no detail too small to recount, no theory too inane to report. But by the middle of the third week there *were* no new details, and even inane theories were running out. So how might the story be kept going?

As if by common consent, various west-country tabloids turned defect to advantage by making the lack of fresh information itself into the story. What were the police doing? How was it that they had no further information on such an infamous crime? Should there not have been an arrest by now? Clearly this was a matter of police "lack of action" that must be addressed.

Superintendent Hanlon called a press briefing. He informed local reporters that he would be demanding more from his officers, conducting a full inquiry into the processes of the investigation, and censuring any negligence he might find.

***

Suiting action to word, Hanlon scheduled his "full inquiry" for the following day. From the view point of those who were its objects, it seemed to consist mostly of a harangue delivered in his office to Cecilia Cavaliere, Verity Jones, and the other officers involved in investigating John Stewart's death. Joseph Stirrup, as having taken part in all the briefings, was also brought in. Hanlon made it clear that he wanted deeds. He wanted people brought in for questioning. He wanted an arrest. He wanted something to happen that could be seen. And, Cecilia reflected, above all what he wanted was something that the *Express and Echo* would characterize as "police chief takes decisive action," or even, perhaps, as "strong man Hanlon takes charge." She further reflected that he had from day one been annoyed at the DCS for putting her in charge of the investigation, and so was happy to seek grounds for criticizing the way it had been conducted.

Whether Cecilia's opinion of the Superintendent's motives was correct or not, it was in any case clear that Hanlon was on a roll. In vain did she point out to him, as politely as she could, that although they had a great deal of information as to what to look for when they found a suspect, they didn't actually *have* a suspect even after questioning everyone in the area. And without more information or witnesses, they had no clear indication as to where to look for one.

Hanlon was having none of it. He had examined the whiteboard, and it was clear to him they were going about the whole thing in entirely the wrong way—just look at DI Cavaliere's comments about the Academy for Philosophical Studies! He turned to her, glaring.

"By all accounts this is an entirely respectable London educational charity that's made notable investment in public educational projects. Who on earth told you this story of an alleged quarrel there?" he demanded.

"I'm sorry, sir, it's a source I can't divulge. But I do trust it."

"In other words, it's unsubstantiated hearsay. Gossip."

Cecilia could feel herself coloring. It was not merely the

professional impropriety of Hanlon's comment: she felt as if Michael Aarons were being called a liar or a gossip, which infuriated her.

She fought to be fair. Of course Hanlon couldn't know whose reliability he was impugning. So she bit her lip and forced herself to go on.

"I *do* trust this source, sir. And the academy's name has also come up in earlier investigations—in the Kakoyannis case in the cathedral. They keep appearing on the fringe of things. Too often to be coincidence, I think."

"But Kakyannis's death was found to be by natural causes, wasn't it?"

"Well, yes sir, but—"

"In which case their appearance there hardly seems to bear on their *alleged* appearance here. DI Cavaliere, do you have a single shred of direct evidence to connect this *respectable educational charity in London* with a small time robbery and murder here in Exeter? Why in heaven's name should you even consider such a preposterous idea?"

Well, of course, she had plenty of evidence, but it wasn't the kind of evidence that she could produce here. Nor, more importantly, was it the kind of evidence that could be used to build a case.

"I'm not concluding anything, sir—as you can see from my comments. I'm just keeping an eye open in their direction."

"Exactly. You're wasting time and energy on that, and in the meantime this whole affair screams at you, burglary-gone-wrong."

"Yes, sir. Unless of course that's just what we're *meant* to think."

"Cavaliere, just because something's obvious, that doesn't mean it isn't so. Much of the time something is obvious simply because that's the way it actually is. I repeat—have you any evidence whatever, any *hard* evidence, that this educational charity might be involved?"

Of course she hadn't. And of course he might be right. Despite her doubts, despite what Michael had been told, there was nothing conclusive. Maybe this *was* just a burglary gone wrong.

"No, sir. Not yet."

"*Not yet!*" He rolled his eyes. "And probably not ever! So for God's sake, *Detective Inspector*, do get on with your job. Start looking where you ought to be looking. Instead of pursuing fascinating theories about people in London who might for some unknown and unspecified reason have had it in for Cox, try questioning the sort of people who are *actually* likely to have done this kind of thing. What about the travelers and the gypsies? How many travelers have you brought in for questioning?"

As it happened, a community of new age travelers had recently linked up with squatters and established itself on property to the west of Exeter, causing fury among local people and being, owing to the peculiarities of English Common Law, fairly difficult to shift legally.

"Travelers?" Cecilia, already rattled, was thrown even further by this new tack. "What have the travelers got to do with it? I've no reason to connect them with this case. By some people's standards they're a scruffy lot, I grant you, and tend to make a mess, but hardly violent. Rather the opposite, most of them."

"Nonsense," Hanlon said. "This is a robbery and a murder. Travelers never stay for long in one place. They have no property except what they move around with. So they're *exactly* the sort of people who might have done this—"

"With all due respect, sir," Verity Jones said, "that's a fallacy."

There was a sharp intake of breath from everyone, including Cecilia. Hanlon glared at Verity, who was elfin today in green and yellow. She gazed back at him, the picture of innocent helpfulness.

"Detective Sergeant Jones," he said, "before you presume to

contradict me, I suggest you take a long and careful look at the facts. The travelers—"

"With respect, sir, it's not a question of facts. I said what you said was a *fallacy*, not a falsity. It's a question of logic."

"What the devil are you talking about, Jones?"

"Well sir, you said, 'travelers don't stay long in one place' and 'travelers don't have any property' and then you said 'so travelers are the sort of people who'd have done this.' But that's not logical—is it sir? The conclusion involves a category that's not in the premises. You might as well say, 'dogs aren't cats' and 'dogs aren't horses' so 'dogs are probably goldfish'. It's a logical fallacy."

Silence.

Hanlon's face grew red.

Joseph Stirrup had a sudden fit of coughing.

Oh Verity, Verity, it's sweet and brave of you to draw his fire, but you're sailing damn close to the wind.

"*Anyone* can chop logic, Jones."

Well no, superintendent, clearly *anyone* can't.

"I'm simply saying, Jones—and I want you all to listen carefully—that we need *results*. And that means hard work. I want to see everyone buckling down, and I want all possible avenues explored. You say you're following up on the boots. But have you followed up on the missing television and the laptop?"

However risky Cecilia might think Verity's diversion had been, it had surely given her a chance to regroup, and her response was prompt.

"We've circulated serial numbers and descriptions," she said, "to every business and person likely to deal with them in the entire Devon and Cornwall area, and we've also notified the Met, Manchester, and the West Midlands. It's all in the report, sir, if you'd like to read it."

"Oh. Well, that's more like it, Cavaliere." For some reason Hanlon seemed suddenly to have run out of steam. "And that's the sort of thing I mean. You see, DS Jones? Real police work.

Well then, keep it up. And remember, we want *results*. Now carry on. Dismissed."

"Yes sir. Thank you, sir."

Cecilia had no idea what was behind the superintendent's sudden deflation, but she raised no question and trooped out with the others.

Perhaps he really had been floored by Verity's telling him his traveler theory was a logical fallacy?

"Verity Jones," Vernon Robbin said as soon as they were out of earshot of the Superintendent's office, "I could kiss you."

Verity Jones looked him up and down.

"Maybe when you're older," she said.

TWENTY-SIX

Heavitree Police Station. A few minutes later.

Superintendent Hanlon sat at his desk, worrying.

The last thing he needed was a call from the academy complaining that the institution or its members were being harassed by people in his own department. Or suppose the chairman came down to complain? He'd met him on a couple of occasions and was not eager to see him again. Or worst of all, suppose there was another visit from his original contact, the man in the Rolls, the one who'd *sniffed* him. The truth was, something about that one terrified him. He hadn't realized when they'd first met in Hendon, when he was a trainee. But this time? When the visit was blessedly over and he got back to the house, he'd realized: he'd been so scared he'd almost wet himself.

So he did *not* want his officers treading on the academy's toes. He was absolutely clear about that.

But then, just now when he'd been challenging Cavaliere about her following up every lead and every piece of information, he'd felt a sudden twinge of guilt. In dissuading her from investigating the academy, shouldn't he have said something about his own links to it? How did his failure to disclose those links fit with his vision of a police force firm and clear in its commitment to procedure, with zero tolerance for deviation from correct protocol in every direction and in all circumstances?

Uncomfortable if not uncertain as to the rightness of what he was doing, he'd dismissed Cavaliere and her minions.

He needed time to think.

To get clear with himself just what he was about.

That was it. The important thing was to be clear.

First, those links to the academy were clearly his business and no one else's. And they gave him his knowledge of the academy, a knowledge that Cavaliere and her colleagues couldn't possibly have. He knew the academy was as concerned as he was to see a Britain that would be united, well organized, disciplined—in fact it was as a part of that concern that they'd seen to his promotion. And through his contact he'd gained a personal knowledge of them in the light of which he could see clearly, as Cavaliere couldn't, that her suspicions of the institution were absurd.

In other words, what had just happened had not been a matter of his avoiding full disclosure. It had simply been a matter of his using his superior knowledge, information to which he alone had access, for the benefit of the entire investigation.

He straightened his shoulders. It was good to be clear in his mind as to what had happened.

Then he frowned.

There was still, of course, the matter of Jones. The stuck up little chit was impertinent. She had irritated him. It came of all that over-education. And Cavaliere encouraged her in it.

The fact was, in his view the entire notion of recruiting university graduates for the police force was misconceived. He was appalled by some recent developments in government policy pointing in that direction. You don't learn policing from books or in a library. You learn it in the university of life.

Well, government policy was a battle for another day.

In the meantime, he knew exactly how to deal with an uppity female detective sergeant. It would take a few days to arrange, but the connection to what had happened this morning would still, he thought, be obvious to everyone. And it would be a disciplinary lesson from which the entire department could benefit.

He reached for his telephone.

TWENTY-SEVEN

London. Monday 18th May.

It had been only a day or two over a week since his appointment to the partnership in the bank and his donation to the academy, but still George felt that he was moving faster than he might have dared hope with respect to both institutions. Twice within the week he'd been invited to cocktail parties at the academy, where pretty hostesses greeted him as Mr. Jameson and handed him Chivas Regal—no water, just a little ice, exactly as he liked it.

He never saw the man from the bar again, the "consultant," nor did he see the vintage Rolls. But at both parties, after he'd stood sipping his Chivas Regal and chatting with the assembled company of mostly businessmen like himself for about thirty minutes, a man in a dark suit—a different man on each occasion—drew him aside. He was then quietly given a piece of information on something about to happen in the world's financial markets—on the first occasion an unexpected rise in the price of a commodity—on the second an unforeseen drop in the price of oil. In each case the advantage this advance knowledge gave him lasted only a few hours, but George had the skills to manage those few hours exceptionally well. As a result, he'd made a great deal of money for his bank and quite a lot for himself.

On the second occasion, moreover, something even more important happened. After his conversation with the man in the dark suit, the Chairman of the academy himself had approached him. George, who had never previously met the tall, distinguished-looking man, was impressed—and flattered, for he was taken into confidence. The academy had some artwork and bullion that needed to be deposited safely, with no questions asked as to their origin or nature. Indeed, the academy would have preferred that they not be in the United Kingdom at all, or even within the European Union, but at present an international move for them was not convenient. Could Gordon and Settlers' oblige, and were they secure?

George was happy to inform the chairman that Gordon and Settlers were discretion itself, and their vaults were as secure as any in the City of London, indeed as secure as the latest constantly reviewed and updated technology could make them.

Within hours the artwork and the bullion arrived, after business hours and in plain vans. It was duly deposited in the bank's ample vaults. Naturally George oversaw the deposit himself.

A strict and sworn condition of the bank's reception of such a deposit was that beyond the routine screening necessary to make sure that it did not contain high explosive or a fissionable device, it would not be examined in any way. Its contents in detail were the depositor's secret.

Naturally, such a sworn promise did not deter George from examining the vault as soon as he had opportunity. He could not for the life of him imagine that the depositors would expect him not to. So far as he could estimate—and he reckoned his estimates were pretty good—the contents included about 500 bars of gold bullion. Each ingot that he examined—he didn't bother to examine them all—bore the eagle stamp of the Third Reich. There were in addition about fifty bags: those he opened at random were stuffed with World War II Reichsmarks. There were also several paintings. After a spot of research he was fairly sure that one of them was a painting of the Virgin by Paolo Veronese that had been looted by the Nazis from a gallery in Bolsano towards the end of the World War II and never recovered by the allies.

All very interesting.

And some indication, surely, as to the origin of the academy's apparently limitless resources.

Very interesting indeed.

Moreover, his having done business with — for? — the Chairman was clearly taking him a step closer to the real center of power, whatever it was.

Even more interesting.

Twenty-Eight

The Academy for Philosophical Studies. The same day.

The chairman was seated alone in his office in an armchair in front of the fireplace. He had so sat for several hours, motionless, gazing down at two oblong boxes that lay on the carpet in front of him.

He was suddenly and unaccountably confused. He had the sense that he was mentally disintegrating. Why was he here? Why was he staring at those boxes? Oh yes. They were things he had made when the consultant told him to... told him how to... now that he was chairman.

But *why* was he chairman? Chairman of what? How had he come to be chairman? There was a huge gap — things he could not remember. There was the first part of his life — his family, his little sister — then there was another part, his career, his time with the party, the war... and then there was the time when it all collapsed in ruins.

But that was years ago. So what had happened since? How had he come to be here? What was the reason?

Ah, now he had hold of it — there *was* no reason. There was no purpose. Reason and purpose were themselves the great mistakes, the grand illusions. *Madam, you rejoiced because the tests were negative and you did not have breast cancer and you are going to be all right. Sir, you rejoiced because the tests were negative and you did not have a heart condition and you will be all right. Fools, both of you. You had a temporary reprieve. That is all. Death is still universal, a hundred per cent certainty. You are not going to be all right. No one is. No one.*

Yes, that was the creed. That at least was clear.

And now, with this recovered clarity in his thinking, he could remember other things, things that happened after the collapse. That was when the consultant came to him. He had told the consultant the things he had come to know, how that the world had no meaning, and how all he had tried to do in the camps was to strip away people's illusions and show them this. And the consultant had said he was glad there were people who thought like that. It was what he had been working for him-self for... for... he could not remember how long the consultant said he had been working, but it was a long time. And then the consultant began working with *him*, teaching him about the life force, the force of nature itself, a force without purpose and without morality — really, just the blind march of life itself towards death. The consultant had taught him how to use that force and then, after decades, at last brought him here.

For their project.

And *that* was why he was chairman. And that was what the boxes were for. And the things in them.

He sighed with relief.

He had it straight again.

The truth was, lately he had begun to have such periods of confusion and disintegration with increasing frequency. They came upon him like a sort of fit, a kind of epilepsy. He must pull himself together. He must get control. Perhaps he should talk to the consultant about it. Perhaps there was a drug he could take.

In the mean time, he had a task to do, a task that would for-ward the project.

He had created the servants. To do this, under the consultant's guidance he had used precisely that force of nature — élan vital, some called it — that the consultant had shown him.

His predecessor, the last chairman, would no doubt have babbled about the Creator's power, and the marvelous irony of using that power to defy Him. He would have spoken of serving another Master — the Destroyer, Iblis, Satan, whatever he chose to call him. But that was all traditionalist nonsense, as useless as black masses and upside-down crucifixes, as irrelevant as morality. There was no Creator and there was no Satan. There was nature. There was the life force. And there was the one final, undeniable, literally all-consuming truth about them both, which was death. The consultant had made it clear he understood that. The consultant had praised him for his realism, the starkness of his views. He relished that praise. All he had ever done, surely, was to show the world the truth of those views, to strip away its illusions.

And now there was the project that would do just that: a catastrophe beyond every catastrophe the world had so far known, a catastrophe that would darken the planet. Giving the two androids life had been the first step. Programming them had been the second, and this too was now complete. They had been returned to him that morning and lay before him in their boxes: dormant, motionless, and ready for dispatch.

But they had never been tested in the field. That, as the consultant said, was an obvious next step, and the chairman would find it amusing. But he needed to present them with a challenge worthy of their powers. And it needed to be in a place where he could observe their performance and their powers of destruction.

He drummed his fingers on the table.

Concentrate. *Concentrate.*

Then again he smiled, entranced by his own sudden clarity of intellect, his ability to think laterally.

Of course! That would be perfect.

He knew just the place.

TWENTY-NINE

Eighty feet below ground in the egg-shaped launch control capsule of control center Alfa-2, Lance Scott sipped his coffee and turned the pages of the Brother Cadfael novel he had been reading for most of the morning—a present from Sophie. "You'll find it a change from Tom Clancy," she said. Somewhat to his surprise, he was enjoying the monkish detective. But then, Sophie surprised him more often than not. He looked at his watch and saw that it was nearly noon—later than he had realized. He and David were already halfway through their twenty-four-hour shift.

He glanced at the two consoles that dominated the capsule. The rows of small green lights looked like those on rather old-fashioned telephone switchboards, only each of these had the words "Strategic Alert" etched across its face. When the lights were on the missiles were ready for launching.

The lights were on now and everything in the capsule was designed to make sure they *stayed* on. Mounted on shock absorbers, its equipment would remain operative even if the earth moved. Internal generators meant that it could produce its own power and rejuvenate its own air. It contained everything that was necessary for basic survival, and more: food, a refrigerator, and a stove; beds, a bathroom, books, a television set, and a radio.

Both the Alfa-1 and Alfa-2 control centers were responsible for ten missiles, a "flight," with a range of up to seven thousand miles and accuracy to within four hundred feet. Each missile carried up to ten independently targetable warheads and each warhead contained twenty-five times the explosive power of the Hiroshima bomb.

No wonder people had been scared when the stuff was first built. No wonder there had been all those *Dr. Strangelove* type movies about the lone maniac who presses the button and starts World War III. Yet in reality there was absolutely no way one person could fire an MX missile.

If an order received over the Primary Alerting System ever seemed like an actual order to launch, then he and David would at once be obliged to open locked red boxes for information that would enable them to verify whether it really came from the President of the United States and the Prime Minister of Great Britain, whose agreement would be required if an American missile were to be launched from British soil. If it did, then what they had received would be an "enable code." Only the President and the Prime Minister had access to these codes, which were contained in boxes carried by military officers who went everywhere that the President and the Prime Minister went.

Their next task would be to dial the code into the console. There were six dials and sixteen figures on each dial, so the possible permutations ran into billions, but without that code the missiles would not be armed and could not fire.

There was yet another safeguard. He and David each had a key. Within one hundred and twenty seconds from the code being entered, the two keys had to be placed in separate keyholes and turned simultaneously. As the keyholes were twelve feet apart it would be impossible for one crewmember to do this alone. When both keys were turned a Launch Vote would be sent out. But then there was still a further check. *Two* Launch Votes were required to launch a missile. So firing a missile actually needed two crews in communication with each other — one in the capsule controlling the flight and one in another capsule — with all four members turning their keys simultaneously: a ten second delay by any one of them would abort the process. Only when all these conditions had been fulfilled *in sequence* would the weapon actually launch. In short, the lone maniac who blew up the world was the stuff of fiction.

The two loudspeakers overhead emitted a sharp, warbling note. Lance laid aside Brother Cadfael and listened. A voice began to broadcast a series of words, slowly and carefully: a female voice, cool, detached, and just slightly insinuating. It was Gianni Turso who'd nicknamed her "Isabella," and the name had stuck. "Isabella," she now was to every controller on the site. "Isabella," warbling softly about her warheads.

Fox-trot, Yankee, Alfa, Tango…

With efficiency born of practice, he and David decoded the message. As on every occasion so far it was routine. But they both knew that an Emergency War Order — a real order to launch — would be broadcast from Strategic Air Command headquarters in exactly the same way. Isabella would be cool, efficient, and impersonal just as today. And she would tell them to fire.

Would he launch the missiles if so ordered? Lance had given the question a good deal of thought. Indeed, those who trained him had insisted he think about it. They had begun by educating him thoroughly in the real horrors of nuclear war. Radiation sickness. Burns. Disease. Then the question had been put to him in a variety of ways: given what he knew of nuclear war, given the inevitable consequences, would he obey an order to launch? His answer had been clear. Yes, he would — because he believed the weapon system he manned to be a genuine deterrent against aggressors, and because a deterrent, if it is to deter, must be real and known to be real. The essential secret of successful warfare, from Marathon to Cannae to Trafalgar to the Gulf, was always the same: have *your* firepower where it can be used to maximum effect against the enemy, and at the same time, by whatever means possible—guile, surprise, sabotage—*prevent* the enemy from using his. The ICBM ensured just that ability.

Of course the work of a missile site was scarcely exciting, and Lance prayed that it stayed that way. Like most truly professional soldiers he did not relish war even when he was winning. His grandfather had been in the habit of quoting the Duke of Wellington on the battle of Waterloo, "The only thing more tragic than victory is defeat." So Lance took seriously the word "Peacekeeper" on the patch sewn to the pocket of his uniform.

But 9/11 had shown that a ruthless and suicidal enemy could *create* its firepower out of the west's own technology. What then of the awful, dreadful paradox that the missiles involved? Could they, too, be used in such a way? "It would take the devil himself to launch those missiles without proper authority," he'd told Sophie over dinner soon after they met. "There's a chain of command, and if it breaks the order isn't valid and the missiles won't launch. Simple as that." His assertion had been as confident as he could make it. "The chain of command," he'd added with a certain pride. "It's vital. That, and acting under lawful authority, are the two things that distinguish a real military from a rabble."

But Lance had long realized that *there was never anything by the wit of man so well devised* (as it said in the front of the old prayer book he used to read under the pew—there being nothing else available—when he was a little boy and bored with the sermon) that some idiot couldn't screw it up. That wasn't, of course, quite how the prayer book put it, but that, as he recalled, was the general idea. And in the world of 9/11, it was clear that there were plenty of idiots willing to do just that.

He sighed and shook his head.

9/11 or not, he could only try to do his job as best he could. "You are the son of a soldier," his grandfather used to say to him if he thought the boy was giving up on something too quickly. "You must hold your position."

As for Sophie? He grinned. In response to his assertion about the safety of the missiles she had merely raised one lustrous black eyebrow in a way that made him want to climb across the table and start making love to her on the spot.

That would certainly have given the waiters in his father's country club something to talk about.

THIRTY

London. Lombard Street. That evening.

The headquarters of Gordon and Settler Merchant Bankers in the heart of London's financial district may not have been as well guarded as R.A.F. Harlsden, but its security was good by most standards and certainly adequate to foil any but the most sophisticated attempt at unauthorized access.

So George, who was working late, found it odd that the red light on his desk had started flashing, indicating that the great bombproof doors of the bank had been opened — opened, moreover, with the correct code, which not even the man on duty knew. Who of the three beside himself with access to that code could possibly be arriving at this hour? He switched on the viewer screen beside his desk. The doors were clearly visible. They stood wide open and through them he could see the blur of moving cars and headlights in the street beyond. He could even hear traffic noises over the sound system.

Beside the doors stood Claypool, the ex-marine on night duty in reception.

"Claypool!" he said sharply, "who was that? And get those damned doors closed, will you! We'll have half London in here if you leave them like that much longer. The main doors should never... Claypool?"

The bank had only recently installed new high definition cameras, and as a result the picture on his screen was good—quite good enough to show him that Claypool was standing in a odd position, one hand slightly raised, fingers pointing slightly forward. He looked as if he had been paralyzed in the act of moving toward whoever had entered.

Paralyzed?

And just who the devil *had* opened the doors?

"*Claypool!*"

It was useless.

He switched to the camera outside the door to his own office, where two more ex-marines were on duty. They were in the act of rising from their chairs. And so they stayed. Paralyzed.

"Garner! Hailsham!"

No reaction.

He began to think he was having a nightmare.

The door to his office crashed inward, splintering and smashing unceremoniously to the floor. Through the dust waddled two small figures, like awkward dolls. Gray, misshapen, ragged, coming towards him.

He sprang to his feet.

Behind them was someone else. Someone tall.

The chairman.

"Good evening, Mr. Jameson," he said, "I have a little surprise for you. You see these androids? Of course you do! Well, we have had them specially programmed for a project the academy has in mind. But I needed to give them a field test. And when you told me all about the marvelous security here, it seemed the ideal place—and you seemed to be the perfect person to experience it. So far, as you can see, the test is going well. It appears that nothing can stop them. Locks. Guards. Nothing. Just as planned! Notice they exercise complete mind control. Your guards are paralyzed, as you will have observed, and when this is over they will remember nothing. Nothing at all."

He *was* having a nightmare. Surely this couldn't be happening?

"For God's sake, Chairman, why are you doing this? I'm on your side! I've done everything the academy asked. The *bank's* done everything you asked!"

"Well, yes. And you have even done one or two things we did not ask, have you not? Did you find inspecting our vault interesting? Of course you did! No need to look embarrassed! You were quite right, you know—we expected you to look. I was well aware what your word was worth. But in any case, so what? So we are *indebted* to you? Oh, Jameson, Jameson, surely you are not going to start talking about *loyalty*, are you?"

Apparently the androids did not trouble to paralyze George as they had paralyzed the guards. He was still wriggling and screaming as he crashed through the plate glass window and flew in a graceful parabola across Lombard Street, becoming silent and still only at the instant when he hit the wall opposite with a messy thump, thence to slither bloodily down it to the pavement three stories below.

THIRTY-ONE

The chairman gazed down with satisfaction at the boxes now safely holding his androids.

They had performed excellently. Indeed, they were just as good as they had been promised to be. The consultant would be well satisfied. The electronics programming had worked perfectly. Best of all, they had evidently not been endowed with any of that reluctance to hurt a human being with which some robotics specialists still insisted on programming their creations. That had been particularly important.

It was perhaps a shame about Jameson, who had been proving quite useful in other ways.

Still, he could easily be replaced. There were plenty more like him.

The chairman got up from his chair, walked across to a cabinet, and poured himself some Perrier water.

He stood, sipping slowly.

And Jameson had also, he must admit, proved amusing—just as the consultant had promised.

How the fellow had screeched and wriggled!

He had found it stimulating.

It brought back the old days. Listening to them squealing in the gas chambers. The last camp he was in had, of course, lacked gas chambers. But then, it had been fascinating to watch what could be achieved through the twin weapons of sickness and starvation. And there was always the option of kicking or beating one of them to death, if one was in the mood for some more active form of satisfaction.

He found it strange how much stimulation most people seemed to find in sex. Sex, in his view, was a much over-rated activity — even rape, though that was certainly more satisfying than the namby-pamby kind, the mere thought of which he found quite disgusting.

But violent death, now, in all its forms — that was arousing.

He paused. Of course one must remember — killing Jameson had not only been pleasant in itself. It had been a reminder of why they were doing this, the purpose of it all.

Still, it made him hope the end would not be *too* quick when it came.

He rather hoped that he would hear shrieks and screams.

See people running about in panic.

Watch them as they lay moaning and dying.

He took another sip of Perrier.

It would be good to end on a high.

THIRTY-TWO

Exeter. Tuesday, 19th May. Evening.

The Cavalieres lived next door to each other, Cecilia in the house her parents had bought for her when she married, and they in the other. But they almost always ate supper together. Tonight it was to be at Andrea's and Rosina's, and they had invited Verity Jones and Joseph Stirrup to join them. Afterwards they planned to watch a film.

It was Papa's turn to choose and he'd picked *The Governess*. They had all seen it before, but Papa said he'd enjoy watching it again because it was such a marvelous portrayal of a completely dysfunctional family. It reminded him of several of his students.

Cecilia said that being Italian he naturally enjoyed watching situations where apparent order was merely a thin disguise for what was in fact complete chaos.

Mama said he had a crush on Minnie Driver.

By six o'clock they were all comfortably installed with dogs, wine, and various *anti-pasti* created on this occasion by Cecilia, ready to watch the BBC news.

The speaker of the House of Commons, who'd been under pressure because of his handling of issues involving MPs' expenses, was to stand down, which made him the first Commons' speaker for three hundred years to be, in effect, forced out of office. The president of the United States had announced tough targets for new fuel-efficient vehicles in order to cut pollution and reduce his country's dependence on foreign oil. A country music singer had announced that she and her best friend's husband were to marry as soon as he could get a divorce.

"Presumably," Verity said, "she means she'll be marrying the *ex*-husband of her *ex*-best friend."

The news turned to crime. There had been a spectacular murder at one of the City's most prestigious banks. During the first part of the segment Cecilia was mainly concerned with seeing that Joseph's and Verity's glasses were properly refilled with the ice cold Vernaccia she'd chosen to serve with her *crostini al mascarpone e noci* and *datteri ripeni di ricotta*. So she did not take much notice. She didn't focus until the newscaster showed the victim's picture and said his name, George Jameson.

"Oh dear God," she said quietly, and sat down.

Joseph and Verity stared at their hosts.

"What's the matter?" Joseph said. Cecilia put up a hand and they all were quiet until the coverage of the murder had finished.

"Do you know him?" Verity said.

Cecilia sighed. "Yes Verity, I suppose you could say I know him. He's my ex-husband."

"Oh, Cecilia, I'm so sorry. This is awful."

"Would you like us to go?"

Joseph was already reaching to unlock the brakes on his wheelchair.

"No! I mean no, please! The man dumped me for someone else and I haven't even seen him now for a couple of years, more, two-and-a-half probably. He called me a few months ago on the phone, I still don't really know why. Anyway, there was a time when it hurt like hell, but I'm over it."

"Our daughter mourned her marriage for well over a year," Andrea said quietly. "And during that time, given means and half a chance, I'd cheerfully have murdered George myself."

Cecilia smiled at him and took his hand.

"Papa, I love you, but you might just want to be careful how often you say that kind of thing around police officers!" She let out a slightly manic giggle. "Trust me! I'm a detective. I know about these things."

"But truly," she added after a moment, in somewhat more sober tone, "I'm over it. I have been for a while. Honestly, I can't remember the last time I even thought about George."

She paused again. "To tell you the truth, at this exact moment, I'm not sure how I'm feeling."

Still holding Papa's hand, she looked up at Mama, who laid a hand on her shoulder. "I mean, I did love George and I slept with George and I made love to George. Would be still, I suppose, if he hadn't pushed off. And it is strange, isn't it? To think he isn't around anymore. Not just not around *me*, but not around *at all*. And that he made someone mad enough at him to kill him. And in such a way. It's… it's weird."

She sighed and shook her head.

"But I do know this. I didn't wish George any ill and I'm really sorry he's met a nasty end. But I'm *not* your grieving widow. In about half an hour Mama's going to produce her *lasagne*, which she's been making all day and is the best in the universe, and *she'll* kill someone if it's not done justice to. So please, stay, and let's eat and drink and watch papa's film and have a nice time. And make me laugh, please. And I dare say tonight I'll go to bed a bit drunk. But believe me, I am *not* about to go into mourning over George Jameson."

"Well I never met George, but I already know one thing about him," Verity said.

"What's that?"

"He was an idiot."

Cecilia raised an eyebrow.

"Any man who dumped you would have to be out of his tiny mind."

"Hear, hear!" Joseph said, reaching for another *crostino al mascarpone*. "You'd be worth hanging on to, even if only for the hors d'oeuvres."

Thirty-Three

Cecilia woke with a headache and a dry mouth.

She lay for several minutes gazing up at the ceiling. The only sounds were Figaro's breathing and the ticking of the eight-day clock in the sitting room.

Despite everything she'd said last night—and meant—about being over George and not caring any more, when she finally got into bed she'd wept, and at last fallen asleep on a pillow damp with tears, dimly aware of Figaro's tail thumping slowly in rhythmic sympathy.

No doubt the wine—she'd drunk rather more than was her habit—had something to do with those tears, but not everything. For even now she ached with sadness as she thought of George. George, always so sure of himself when it came to ways of the world, always full of energy and ideas—absurd or not. George, running a bit to fat but vain enough to pull his stomach in when he thought about it. George…

It was not, exactly, that she wanted him back. God knows she'd grieved when he left. But life had gone on, and over months and then years her pool of hurt had dwindled to a puddle and finally dried up. And now? She hadn't cried for *him*, not really—what she'd cried for, what saddened her, was the appalling futility of it all. In this bed they'd laughed. In this bed they'd loved. They'd made promises and plans. Yet in the end it all meant nothing. It had been for nothing.

She sighed.

Then she frowned, shook her head, and sat up.

The plants needed watering.

And Figaro needed his walk and his breakfast.

When she got out of the bathroom twenty or so minutes later there was already a message on her mobile directing her to a break-in at a securities firm on the other side of Exeter. Dealing with that proved complicated, not least because of the inadequacy of the firm's own security systems, which had been inspected and declared satisfactory by a police inspection team only three weeks ago, and now turned out to have been anything but.

Which was awkward, to say the least.

"But then," DS Robbin said when the full extent of the disaster had become clear, "who could possibly have imagined the thieves would go all high-tech and state-of-the-art on us like this?"

Cecilia raised an eyebrow and stared at him.

"*We* could have imagined it, Detective Sergeant," she said at last. "It's what they pay us for."

So what with one thing and another, it was not until mid-morning that she arrived at the Heavitree Road police station.

The first thing she noticed was a gleaming black Mercedes S-Class parked outside the main entrance. Indeed, she could hardly avoid noticing it since it was parked semi-diagonally and half a meter out from the curb—"not so much parked as abandoned" she muttered to herself as she pulled around it to get to her own part of the car park.

The second thing was a little scene in the opposite corner of the lot. Verity Jones was putting a cardboard box into the boot of her car, and Joseph was sitting by in his wheelchair with another box on his lap. They did not look happy.

She parked in her usual place, and then walked over to them. Verity looked as if she had been crying. Joseph looked near to tears himself.

"What's the matter?" Cecilia asked.

Verity took a photograph of her parents and a photo of Magdalen College, Oxford, from the box on Joseph's knee and put them into the back of the car.

Cecilia looked at Joseph.

"It's f — — — Hanlon," he burst out.

Cecilia was stunned. In the time she'd known Joseph she couldn't recall him even saying "damn" until now.

"He's had Verity transferred."

"*What?*"

"To Barnstaple."

"He says I need a change of experience," Verity said.

"What on earth are you going to do in *Barnstaple*?"

"Try to be the best police officer I can." Her jaw was set, but her voice quivered slightly.

Cecilia looked from Verity to Joseph and back to Verity.

"Detective Sergeant Verity Jones," she said, "you're already a damn good officer and probably the most logical brain we've got here in CID. And everyone in this station knows it."

Verity stopped loading her belongings and looked at her.

"Thank you, ma'am. Coming from you that means a lot. And Joseph and I know this isn't your fault, and there's not a thing you can do about it."

Cecilia stepped close and gave Verity a quick hug and a kiss on each cheek.

"Oh ma'am — protocol!"

"Damn protocol." She stepped back. "Take care, Verity. If there's anything I *can* do to get you back here where you belong, I'll do it. And make sure you stay in touch."

She left them.

THIRTY-FOUR

Heavitree Road Police Station, a few minutes later.

"It's a bloody disgrace," Sergeant Wyatt said as Cecilia entered the station. From his position at the desk he had a clear view of the car park, and there was little doubt what he was talking about.

"Sergeant," she said, "I couldn't agree with you more."

What she was about to do was crazy and might well ruin her own career. She was so angry she didn't care. She went straight to the glass-paned door of Superintendent Hanlon's office, opened it without knocking, walked past his secretary, opened the door to Hanlon's inner sanctum, again without knocking, and entered.

He was at his desk examining what appeared to be a letter.

As she entered he looked up, plainly startled, and immediately put his hand over the letter. Clearly he didn't want her to see it.

She walked up to his desk and looked down at him.

"Superintendent Hanlon, why have you transferred one of our best officers, who's in the middle of a case—a case that's my responsibility, a case you've emphasized you want results on—without even bothering to consult me?"

Hanlon leaned back in his chair.

"There's no need to come barging in here, Cavaliere, or to take that tone. I've decided Jones needs a different kind of experience, and I'm not answerable to you for my decisions. I'll thank you to remember that. Now go—and shut the door on your way out."

"No, sir, you are not answerable to me," Cecilia said without moving. "But the fact remains we all know exactly why you transferred Detective Sergeant Jones. It's because she's bright and she's lippy and she cheeked you. Actually, she didn't just cheek you, did she? She showed up your prejudice for the irrational nonsense it is. That's the advantage of knowing how to *chop logic*, I suppose."

"Jones's problem, Cavaliere, is too much education. You don't seem able to see that. Good policing is learned in the university of life, not out of books in a college library. Real *life*, Cavaliere—where it doesn't all work out according to logic and things are tough and there are real criminal types who commit real crimes and really hurt people and really kill them and have to be stopped. And that's what we're supposed to be doing, Cavaliere. And stopping them means getting *results*, not chasing theories about logic."

"Oh, really, sir! Real life's tough, is it? Well, sir, I never knew that. Thank you so much for telling me. And people really get killed, do they? I'll try to remember that. And as for *results*? Well, in that Cumberland House murder they're bound to be a bit slower now, aren't they, since you've taken one of our best minds off the case, even if she is a bit *overeducated*. And, incidentally, you've badly upset one of our other best minds. I'm sure he'll go on doing what he can, but losing DS Jones is bound to impair his performance a bit."

"If you mean that computer fellow in the basement—"

"That computer fellow in the basement works for you, sir, and he has a name."

"I know that, Cavaliere. It's… Stripe, of course, but—"

"His name's Stirrup, sir. Joseph Stirrup."

"Cavaliere, there are dozens of people working in this station, and I don't pretend to know the name of every civilian assistant. I am, however, aware of more that's going on here than you imagine, and one thing I'm aware of is an entirely unsuitable relationship developing between Jones and Stripe — I mean Stirrup — which is another excellent reason for her to have a change of scene."

"Isn't the suitability of their relationship rather up to them to decide, sir? It doesn't seem to be impairing their work. Rather the opposite, from what I've seen."

"Cavaliere, if you can't see why that relationship is unsuitable, I don't know how to explain it to you."

"Really, sir. Well let *me* try. Would it be because he's black? Or because he's a cripple? Or maybe both? Of course, merely being black and crippled, he wouldn't know about life being tough, would he? Perhaps you ought to tell him about it."

Hanlon pushed his chair back and came abruptly to his feet. His face was white with anger.

"Cavaliere, I didn't ask for this interview and I damned well resent your putting words in my mouth."

For an instant Cecilia thought he was going to strike her, and in the madness of her own anger she wished he would, giving her reason to strike him back. But he merely glared and she glared back, and so they stood at an impasse.

"Well then, sir," she said finally, "don't worry about it, because I've absolutely nothing more that I want to say to you." Her voice was still low but perfectly clear. She started to turn away.

"I haven't told you to leave yet."

She turned back to face him.

"Cavaliere, I gather some people seem to think you've done some useful work round here, and perhaps you have. But just remember, you are not indispensable."

"Well, sir, I'm very glad to hear that. And you *did* tell me to leave, several minutes ago."

She turned on her heel and left, pausing on her way out only to give Hanlon's secretary her most dazzling smile.

THIRTY-FIVE

Heavitree Police Station. A few minutes later.

B ack in her office, Cecilia sat at her desk and reflected that neither office nor desk was likely to be hers much longer. She gazed at the photograph of Mama and Papa. Maybe she'd better go and find a cardboard box.

Then she shrugged.

She wasn't fired yet, so until the bombshell landed she might as well get on with her job. She opened the file on this morning's burglary and started to work on it.

Only occasionally did her mind wander back to Verity.

It occurred to her that Hanlon's problem with Verity probably stemmed from that time soon after she started her job, when he tried to grope her in the hall outside his office.

In other words, she'd allow Joseph to touch her but she wouldn't allow Hanlon. That would surely irritate a man like him.

Well, it just showed Verity knew who was the better man, didn't it?

Back to work.

After a minute or so she looked up again, frowning.

What on earth was that letter or whatever on Hanlon's desk?

She wouldn't have noticed it at all if he hadn't made such a business of covering it with his hand.

Odd, that.

Not that she really cared.

Back to work.

As it happened, Superintendent Hanlon had already decided that for the moment, at least, he could aim no bombshell at DI Cecilia Cavaliere, however much he might want to.

He was angry but he was not a fool.

Verity Jones—funny, hardworking, and good-natured—was respected and popular. Hanlon was well aware how much resentment his removing her had caused. And that had been precisely the point. So what if Cavaliere was right, and everyone knew why he'd transferred Jones? Well then, good. The message ought to be clear. He was a man who would brook no nonsense or insolence from anyone, and in particular he would not put up with insolence from young women already promoted above their abilities. Let those who perceived this learn from it, and beware.

Goddammit, he wished he could move Cavaliere, too. All right, her track record was excellent, but her performance in the Culberton House murder so far was also typical of her weaknesses: a lot of thrashing about and cleverness accompanied by a simple failure to tackle the obvious suspects—and people like travelers *were* the obvious suspects, however much people might choose to show their cleverness and their social sensitivity by arguing otherwise. Yes, they could talk about "profiling" and condemn it with high-sounding words about justice and individual human rights—and God knows, Hanlon was as concerned as the next man about individual rights. But the fact was, there was a *reason* for profiling: *it often worked*. Simple as that.

The problem was, Cavaliere too was popular and respected.

Even Sergeant Wyatt, whom he'd have expected to be supportive of old-fashioned values, seemed to think the sun shone out of her backside. And not only that—unlike Jones, Cavaliere seemed also to have support in high places. It was, after all, the chief constable herself who'd insisted on promoting her to the rank of detective inspector in the face of Hanlon's vehement objection. So he needed to be careful. It would not be wise to stoke up any more anger against himself at the station. Nor was he at all sure what Cavaliere would do if he attempted to remove her.

In the course of his career he'd said all the politically correct things about the importance of women for good policing and so on. Such compromises were necessary if one was to get anywhere these days. But the fact was, women introduced a degree of triviality and woolly-mindedness into any undertaking of which they were part, police work included, and the creeping rot was already visible everywhere he looked. The Jones girl as a detective sergeant in CID was an appalling example—no wonder the public was losing confidence in the force. What were they supposed to think when they called for aid and a dolled-up little chit like that arrived? There was a time when she'd have been lucky to make typist. So her removal from the Heavitree station was a step, at least, in the right direction. He only wished he could have demoted her at the same time.

As for Cavaliere, there must be *something* he could do.

With that thought he turned his attention to the letter on his desk with its heavily embossed letterhead on bond paper. It had arrived hand delivered from the academy that morning and contained, as the tall man had promised, his instructions. He did not entirely understand what their purpose was, but they seemed simple enough. Perhaps when he'd carried the instructions out, when he'd done what the tall man asked, perhaps then the academy would help him do something about Cavaliere?

Possibly she *could* be removed from her position, once his own position was more secure.

That would make sense.

But it also meant being patient.

He would throw no bomb for the present.

So Hanlon did nothing.

And so nothing happened.

Save that from now on he and Cecilia Cavaliere both understood that they were enemies.

THIRTY-SIX

"It seems to me," David Levi said, "that far too many people get married anyway, and half of them do it because they feel they ought to. Peer pressure. Or parent pressure. And the result's a huge amount of human misery. In my opinion nobody ought to get married unless they're absolutely sure they couldn't possibly imagine going on with their lives *without* marrying whoever it is. Period."

"I'm inclined to agree with you." This from John, a stocky, cheerful major. "I should know — I've been married three times already. If you want it to stick, you need to be sure. And I mean *damn* sure."

"Were *you* sure?"

"Sure I was sure. Every time!" He chuckled.

"Well, yes…" David hesitated.

Lance swallowed a smile. John had unwittingly blown a large hole in part of David's argument, and David was quite smart enough to see it.

"Yes, well, right," he said at last, "even feeling sure isn't going to guarantee anything. But I still say it's the least you need."

He sipped his gin and tonic.

"The fact is, once upon a time we used to value maiden aunts and bachelor uncles. Now we just assume they must be gay."

"What if they are?" Lance asked.

"I'm not making a point about gays. Gays are fine. I'm simply saying that a lot of middle class America seems no longer able to imagine that an ordinary heterosexual male or female might actually lead quite a happy, useful, and productive life *without* being married."

"No doubt the military's hard on marriage." This was Gianni Turso, who could speak on the subject with some authority, being thoroughly and successfully married himself, with five bouncing children to prove it.

"Well, I guess that's true." David grinned. "And maybe it influences my thinking more than I care to admit. The fact is, I do like being free to volunteer for interesting jobs without losing sleep worrying over somebody back home. I like being free to make relationships where I can. And I certainly don't want somebody back home losing sleep worrying about me."

Lance held his peace—aware, even if the others had not noticed, that it was at his prompting that the conversation had turned into these channels. Sophie's latest letter had arrived this morning, and with it she'd sent a photograph of herself looking fabulous at somebody's wedding. Letter and photo were in his pocket now.

He couldn't get her out of his head. Didn't want to, for that matter. He liked his happy, interesting life with Sophie in it. And why not?

He was dead in love with her.

And he was pretty sure she loved him.

If they married, though, they'd be an odd pair by almost any reckoning.

She was second violinist with the Chicago Symphony.

He was Air Force, and knew about as much about music as she knew about missiles.

Her parents, also musicians, were second generation immigrants from Greece.

On his side, there had been a Scott in the armed forces of the United States since 1837, the only exception being the years before the country entered World War II, during which his grandfather had served with the R.A.F. in 71 Squadron of the famed American Eagles, flying for King George against the Führer. His Royal Air Force cap and wings, and a black and white photograph of him — handlebar mustache and all — standing by his Spitfire Mk. V were still among Lance's most treasured possessions.

Sophie's family always voted Democrat.

His were lifelong Republicans — or at least had been until the last Republican presidency, which had so disgusted them they were now not sure what they were.

Sophie's family was Greek Orthodox.

His was Episcopalian.

She liked to discuss everything.

He didn't.

Not only did none of this seem to bother her, she appeared to find it all extremely interesting. But it certainly threatened the hell out of him.

And of course she'd picked up on that.

"You don't want *me*," she said to him one day quite early in their relationship. "You really don't. I'm just not the Air Force officer wife type. *Look* at all the officers' wives, Lance. I'm nothing like them."

"I *have* looked at them," he said, "They don't interest me."

"Oh, really," she said, and raised that infuriating and entrancing eyebrow. "Then what *does* interest you?"

The answer to that was obvious.

But then it implied the next question, which on his last visit home had been put bluntly to him by his mother — herself an officer's wife to her core, though she and Sophie seemed to have hit it off amazingly well.

"So what are you going to do about it?" his mother said.

"Do about what?"

His mother raised one eyebrow.

Damn it, he'd never seen her do that before. Was it *catching*? Wasn't imitation the sincerest form of admiration? Good grief, the last thing he needed in his life just at present was a Sophie-mother *axis*.

Oh, hell.

THIRTY-SEVEN

The same day. Late evening.

Cecilia had given Figaro and her parents' dogs their last walks of the day and returned Tocco and Pu to her parents. She and Figaro now stood on the pavement outside their house, enjoying the night air for a few moments before going home. She was feeling much better than she had earlier, for two reasons.

First, when she told her parents what had happened at work, Papa—naturally able to view the situation in a more detached way than she could—was quite sure that however angry Hanlon might be, he would do nothing. "Everyone knows you're an excellent officer with an outstanding record. Hanlon has no reason to offer for undermining your position save your having criticized his reasons for removing Verity Jones from her duties. And since she too is an excellent officer, that reason once known could well turn out to be far more embarrassing to him than to you. He knows that. He won't do a thing."

Second, Verity had telephoned to say she'd found pleasant digs with a nice family in Barnstable, her new colleagues were kind and welcoming, and she was sure being there would be a useful experience for her, just like the Superintendent said.

"*Lei è una ragazza brava!*" Mama said after the call, and Cecilia agreed: she was a brave girl, and making the best of it. Joseph also had telephoned. Having talked to Verity on the phone and heard that she was settling in, he was clearly calmer and feeling better.

So now she and Figaro stood together for a moment savoring the fresh night air.

"Woof," Figaro said informatively, wagging his tail and pointing.

A figure in a black cloak was walking towards them. As he drew nearer Cecilia could make out his face: dark hair touched with gray, dark bearded, a little past his youth. He was evidently a priest.

"Good evening, Father," she said as he came level with her.

"Good evening," he said. "A pleasant one. Detective Inspector Cavaliere, I think? Cecilia Anna Maria Cavaliere."

"I am," she said. "And you are?"

"I am Friedrich Spee. Friedrich Spee von Langenfeld."

"Are you on the staff of the cathedral, Father?"

"In spirit only." He smiled. "I greet you in the name of our Lord Jesus Christ — as they would, I am sure. But I am a member of the Society of Jesus. A Jesuit."

"Oh, I beg your pardon."

"Not at all. Over the centuries I have become a great admirer of *ecclesia Anglicana*. Not all Catholics feel they must pick the flowers in other people's gardens."

She smiled back. He had an odd way of speaking — *over the centuries?* — but he struck her as a good man. And an interesting one.

"Are you new to Exeter, then? I don't think I've seen you before."

"I am… visiting. It's beautiful — quite different from Germany as I knew it, but beautiful."

"How long have you been here?"

"Just a short time."

"Oh. Then may I ask how you know who I am?" she said.

"I was told," he said. "Actually, I was sent to warn you. Perhaps even to encourage you."

"I don't understand, Father."

"Of course not," he said. "Forgive me. Why should you? And I am not to tell you too much. But I may tell you this—in the case you're investigating, you're right not simply to believe what seems obvious about the murder of John Stewart Cox. And you are right to be concerned about your old enemy, the Academy for Philosophical Studies. But there is more and worse here than you know. Continue to watch, Cecilia Anna Maria. Watch and pray. That's all for the present. A time will come, quite soon I think, when we shall speak again. In the meantime, talk with your family about this and also with your friend Michael Aarons. He will help you. You will help each other. And please warn him. There will be work for him, too."

How on earth did he know all this? Obviously, he must know Michael.

Spee looked away from her for a moment, toward the city center, as if he had heard something. Then he looked back at her.

"I see," he said, "that you have become a believer. Not that you or your family were ever really *un*believers."

This might have been frightening, but somehow it wasn't. She shook her head.

"Not much of a believer, I'm afraid," she said. "I hardly ever get to mass."

He smiled. "Child, I too was *not much* of a believer, and I went to mass more times in a week than I dare say you can imagine going to in a month. There *is* a connection between the liturgy and sanctity, but it's not nearly as straightforward as some people like to think."

"I'm a bit of a skeptic."

His smile broadened and brightened.

"You are a *doubter*—like Saint Thomas. That's to say, you

aren't credulous, which is, I should have thought, rather a good thing in a police detective. But a skeptic? I think not. I saw you in the cathedral. At the requiem for John Stewart Cox."

"You were there?"

"I saw you. You have much to learn, as have we all, but you are a believer. Let no one deceive you about that. And especially do not deceive yourself." Again he looked towards the city center. "Now I must leave you. I shall remember you in my prayers. God bless you, daughter."

Figaro gave another conversational woof and wagged his tail. The priest smiled and leaned down to scratch his head.

"Yes, and you too, my small friend. You are close to our Beloved, as are all your kind. And who knows what you will do?"

He stood, smiled again at Cecilia, and walked on.

She gazed after him, as astonished by the way he left her as she was by the whole encounter. One moment he was walking away from her, only a few feet away. The next moment he disappeared — dissolved, almost — into the gloom cast by the trees. Were it not for Figaro she might think she had imagined the whole thing. But Figaro continued to look in the direction in which the priest had gone and to wag his tail, so Figaro certainly seemed to think he was real enough.

After a few moments she sighed and shook her head, then turned towards the house.

But Figaro, continued looking towards the trees and wagging his tail, and did not cease either of these activities until he and Cecilia were actually inside, with the front door closed and much on Cecilia's mind.

THIRTY-EIGHT

Heavitree Road Police Station. The following morning.

When Cecilia arrived in her office at a few minutes after eight the following morning she was still puzzling over her encounter with the mysterious Father Spee.

But immediately her thoughts were taken in another direction by a voice message from Joseph. As soon as she had time, could she please come to him in the boffins' underground kingdom? He needed to show her something he thought she'd want to know about.

She went down to him right away.

"Ma'am," he said, "look at this."

On the computer screen was a page from the digital edition of the *Hackney Gazette*. At the center of it was a photograph of a group of men.

Joseph pointed to the date.

"Day before yesterday," she said.

"Right."

She read the caption under the photograph: *Visiting Members of the Academy for Philosophical Studies in Bayswater Pose Outside the Cranston College of Technology*. She read the beginning of the article.

"It says they were there to inspect progress in the repairs and rebuilding following the recent collapse at the site." She looked at Joseph. "Is this from the program you arranged for Verity?"

"She asked me to keep an eye on her stuff, and that's what came up."

"So the academy is back in business with Cranston College."

"Yes, ma'am, apparently it is. But that's not really what I want you to look at. You see, this is really a good photograph. Much better than you might expect."

He framed a section and enlarged it.

"And it's especially good when we give it a little help with the digital enhancer."

He pressed a couple of keys.

"And presto."

"Good heavens!"

"Yes, ma'am."

Joseph didn't need to point it out to her.

Gazing at them from the computer screen was handsome, curly-haired Superintendent James Hanlon.

"Throws a new and interesting light on his trying to steer us all away from investigating the Academy for Philosophical Studies, doesn't it, ma'am?"

It certainly did.

Cecilia walked slowly back to her office.

Here was a surprise. A rather nasty surprise.

And there was still the question of Father Spee.

Spee knew something of her previous encounters with the academy. He'd asked her to talk to Michael. To *warn* him, in fact. *There will be work for him, too.* What work? How did he know Michael? They were both priests. Perhaps Michael had told him about the academy? That would make sense.

The Jesuit said someone had sent him. Who?

Still, he'd suggested she talk to Michael. And to Papa and Mama.

She'd do that.

She wasn't entirely sure why, but when she was talking to Michael she always felt safe and happy.

Which was odd, really, since a lot of the chances she'd had to spend time with him had been in situations of some stress.

And at least once, of considerable danger.

THIRTY-NINE

Saint Andrew's, Holborn Circus. That evening.

The telephone rang.

Michael put down volume one of C. K. Barrett's *International Critical Commentary* on the Book of Acts, reached over a cat, and picked up the handset.

"St. Andrew's, Holborn Circus. This is Michael Aarons."

"Hello, Michael. I'm afraid it's me again. Do you have a minute or two? I've got a rather odd development to tell you about. In fact, I've got two odd developments. Both of them *extremely* odd!"

He smiled. Even with someone he enjoyed talking to much less than Cecilia, he'd surely have been unlikely to brush aside such an introduction to a conversation as that.

"Absolutely," he said, "I love odd. In fact, the odder the better."

Cecilia's story of the mysterious Jesuit who had talked with her last evening left him mystified. He didn't recall knowing a Father Spee,

"But," he said, "I do go over to Farm Street quite often."

"Farm Street?"

"The Church of the Immaculate Conception. It's the Jesuit Church. I go to see my spiritual director. So I suppose I could have met Father Spee there. He certainly sounds as if he knows me! But I must admit I'm blanking on him for the moment. What did he look like?"

"Well, of course it was dark. But medium build, dark hair with a bit of gray, dark eyes, dark beard—and a gentle, rather sad manner, as if he'd seen things he'd rather not see. But then also, a lot of authority—I mean, when he said something, you felt he knew what he was talking about. Is this helping any?"

"It's an excellent description—so good it makes it even odder that I don't remember him. He sounds like someone I *would* remember. Let me think about it."

When she told him about Joseph's discovery, he was as surprised as she to learn of the academy's connection to Superintendent Hanlon.

"I want to be fair," Cecilia said, "I mean, I loathe the man, and he's treated one of my friends despicably, but that hardly makes him a monster. So maybe he's just another dupe who doesn't really know what the academy's about."

"Maybe. And maybe not. As your friend Joseph said, it certainly puts his trying to steer you away from them in a different light. I hate to say it of anyone, but for the moment, as far as this business is concerned, I think we have to regard him as the enemy."

"I already do, Michael—though my reasons seem almost petty compared to involvement with the academy."

"Well, then," Michael said, "let's go back to your Jesuit. Despite his odd behavior you were impressed by him, which is one point in his favor. And Figaro seemed to like him, which is another. He told you to watch and pray, which can hardly be bad advice under any circumstances. And you're to warn me I may have to act. Well, you've done that." He sighed. "He's obviously got some good information from somewhere, so maybe he has a good reason for wanting us to know about it. I think for the time being we've just got to do what he said— which isn't a lot."

They explored the question from various angles but could get no further than Cecilia's promise to let Michael know if and when anything else happened, and Michael's promise to ask his friends in Farm Street who Father Spee was.

Their business was done, but it seemed that neither wanted the conversation to end. So they talked of Jane Austen, "a pillar of sweet reason and good nature in an insane world," Michael said.

Cecilia liked that.

He'd had been rereading *Northanger Abbey*. "How about John Thorpe as the original sleazy second-hand salesman?" he said.

For some reason Cecilia found that funny. She giggled about it, then made a reference to Sleazy Thorpe a few minutes later and started giggling again.

Indeed, half an hour after she had put the phone down, as she was putting Figaro's lead on to take him for his last walk of the day, she was still giggling.

FORTY

Lance Scott threw his bag into the MG and got in himself, ready to go back to his digs in Exeter. David, who was doing extra duty to make up for some he'd missed last week, was not with him.

He put the key in the ignition but didn't turn it.

He sat, thinking. Thinking of Sophie, as he tended to do most of the time these days when he wasn't actually obliged to be thinking about something else.

On one level he knew she was right. His whole picture of what his marriage and his life as a husband might be like was built on assumptions that went with those officer's wives she'd talked about. Nothing wrong with them, of course. Sophie was the first to say that. Nothing wrong with them at all—if that's who you were. But she wasn't. Officers' wives, for example, always put their husbands' careers first, everything else second. And officers' wives asked no questions. But Sophie? It wasn't that she wouldn't try to be helpful. But she'd *always* ask questions. She'd ask questions if you were about to shoot her. She'd want to know how the gun worked. Or what kind of bullets you were using. She was always so... so... so damned... *interested* in everything. And sharp. Was she sharp!

And that, of course, brought him to the real problem. Her mind fascinated him almost as much as everything else about her fascinated him. She continually surprised him. But how on earth could he stop her from becoming bored with him?

"I don't know why you date me," he'd said once. "I guess I'm just your typical simple soldier. I'm totally predictable. I don't know much about music and I'm certainly not a great creative intellect."

"No, I guess you're not," she said. "But you respect intelligence. You're actually a lot more intelligent than you think. And you're a nice man, a good man. I feel safe and happy with you and the truth is I quite like your being predictable. I mean, I think you're predictably honest. And predictably kind and chivalrous. I think you keep your word. And of course I think you're *very* sexy."

Well that was something. But then what would happen when the hormones stopped jumping around?

"As for music, at least you seem to like the noise music makes. We're enjoying the noises together. That's a start."

Nice. Honest. Kind. He hoped so.

He'd even enjoyed the concert, which made him all but burst with pride in her. He kept wanting to tell everyone seated around him, "Hey, you see the gorgeous violinist with short black hair? *I'm taking her out to supper after the show!*"

The truth was he adored her with a strength of feeling so utterly disturbing that at times he found himself almost wishing he'd never known her. Almost, but not quite: for though he had once been well enough content with the peace she had ruined, the turmoil she now gave him made that same peace seem barren and sterile, the calm of a featureless desert. He could not go back to it. He had reached a stage where he could hardly bear to think what it would be like to live without her. He guessed on that count he met Jim's criterion for marriage.

But could he live *with* her? Or, more precisely, could she live with him, year in and year out, without being bored mindless?

There were times when the thought of what might happen to them terrified him.

But then—

Footfalls echo in the memory

Down the passage which we did not take

Towards the door we never opened

Into the rose garden.

That thought was terrifying too.

He sighed, shook his head, and turned the key in the ignition. The engine turned at once and fired sweetly. He smiled.

That part of his life, at least, seemed to be running smoothly.

FORTY-ONE

St. Andrew's, Holborn Circus. Monday, 25ᵗʰ May. 10.00 a.m.

Michael Aarons sat at his desk signing various legal papers connected with Diocesan church plate.

"Here you are, Father, nice and strong. Just like you like it."

"Thank you, Mrs. Marshall."

"Mrs. Owens says to say she knows you don't usually have a biscuit with your morning cup of tea, but she sent you one this morning 'cause they're fresh baked—just out the oven."

"It looks delicious. Thank you. Mmm. Yes. *Very* good. My congratulations to Mrs. Owens."

"And Mrs. Owens says if it's all right with you we'll do the sitting room first today before the bedrooms, because of you having them bishops in later."

"Does Jim know?"

"Yes, Father. Fact is, he suggested it."

"Well, then, tell Mrs. Owens that will be fine."

"Thank you, Father."

Mrs. Marshall scurried away, and Michael returned to the church plate. He signed a paper. Signed another one and thought how much more he enjoyed talking with Cecilia Cavaliere than... well, anything else he could think of. He recalled the times he'd been with her. Cecilia coolly disarming a murderous assassin. Cecilia rescuing a ladybird. Cecilia reading her map under a light. Cecilia Anna Maria, as he now knew her to be—for he'd looked her up on the Internet and discovered her whole beautiful name.

But why—how—was the academy connected with Cecilia's superintendent? And how had Father Spee the Jesuit come to be involved? The more Michael thought about that, the more he almost convinced himself he *must* have met the man on one of his visits to Farm Street. And perhaps talked to him about the academy. He'd already tried calling Farm Street to see if someone there knew a Father Spee, but everyone he knew seemed to be away and none of them would be back for several days. He did manage to speak to a sister who checked their visitors' book for him and also some kind of local register but came up with nothing.

Damn.

In the meantime, Spee had said, "Watch and pray."

Well, if anyone could watch, Cecilia could.

So presumably his job was to pray.

FORTY-TWO

Cecilia had visitors. A detective chief inspector and detective sergeant from the Metropolitan Police. They'd come about George, and their visit was no more than she'd been expecting. If anything she was surprised it hadn't come sooner. They had, after all, a baffling murder on their hands, and she was the victim's ex-wife. If she'd been involved in it in some way or even planned the whole thing, she'd hardly have been the first ex-wife to connive at the murder of a treacherous ex-husband.

So she sat them down in her office, offered them tea (which they politely declined), and prepared to cooperate as best she could.

Her impression of the interview was that no one really imagined she'd had anything to do with George's murder. They were merely checking all leads, as they were bound to. But then, just as she was beginning to feel they must have covered pretty well everything that could be covered, the DCI came up with something that surprised her.

"Would you happen to know anything about the details of your ex-husband's bank account?"

"I'm sorry, I'm afraid I don't."

"Well, George Jameson recently made a large payment to an educational charity in London. And he recently became a member of its governing board."

She felt the back of her neck prickle. She knew what he was going to say next.

"It was a group called the Academy for Philosophical Studies."

From her, a sharp intake of breath.

"You know something about them?"

"As a matter of fact I do, though I didn't know George had any connection with them." She paused. He gave an encouraging cough, and waited. "Look, I've nothing against them that I could press, no hard evidence of a crime. I wish I had. But I do have suspicions about them, and if this were my case their connection with George is certainly something I'd want to look into. As it happens, I cautioned a couple of your colleagues about them some time ago" — here she gave him the names — "and perhaps you should talk with them. They may by now have better information than I."

He thanked her. Of course they would follow up on her suggestion and let her know if there were any developments.

He closed his notebook, glanced at his watch and then at his colleague, who looked hopeful.

"We're finished a bit sooner than we expected, Detective Inspector." He smiled. "So if the offer's still open, we'll take those cups of tea."

FORTY-THREE

The Academy for Philosophical Studies. The same day.

Monday at the academy started much like any other Monday.

Then, at about nine-fifteen a.m., a fifty-inch satellite television arrived for the chairman's office. No one knew why it was wanted, but those who delivered it clearly had the chairman's authorization, so the set was unloaded and duly installed.

Midway through the morning the chairman himself arrived. He announced that for the rest of the day he was not to be disturbed, and retired to his office, closing the imposing mahogany door behind him.

"He didn't even get his messages," one of the secretaries said.

"Presumably he wants to watch TV all day," Tom Weaver said.

Inside his dimly lit office the chairman stood for a moment gazing round. The curtains were drawn as usual, and the walls flickered as usual in light from the fire. In the center stood the television, its slim lines and twenty-first-century design contrasting oddly with the ornate Edwardian vulgarity that surrounded it.

When the missiles landed on Moscow, Teheran, Beijing, and

Pyongyang, the news channels would surely show something of it. That was why the television was there.

And as soon as the missiles had been detected — which would surely happen moments after they were launched — those who were targeted would surely have launched their own retaliation, which would arrive within minutes of the western missiles hitting their targets.

He walked over to a cabinet and poured himself a glass of Perrier. He took a few sips, put aside his glass, and crossed the room.

The drapes were dark and heavy, and nobody ever drew them. Twice he jerked at the cord without effect, but at his third effort, something gave. Slowly, as if reluctant, the heavy velvet moved back, and pale sunlight flooded the green and gold room, revealing that it was not only vulgar, but also shabby, and not particularly clean: there were cobwebs hanging from the ceiling. Through the window, across the street, he could see terraced houses like the one he was in; to his right, Hyde Park. For several minutes the chairman stood and stared at the distant tree line.

Then he smiled. Of course if the Bayswater Road proved to be ground zero, he would see nothing. Merely experience the exquisite annihilation. But perhaps when Moscow or Beijing, or most probably both, retaliated as they surely would, he might see from this window some of the missiles come in, and experience at first hand several moments of London's dying agony and the terror that would accompany it, before the holocaust engulfed him.

This, indeed, was his hope. With the consultant's aid, he had taught himself to desire a dark mystery: death, the only ultimate truth of an otherwise meaningless universe. He had taught himself to desire it not only for himself but for all. He would therefore lay down his life with an intention precisely opposite to that alleged of Him who had laid down his life upon the cross.

The chairman looked up as the clock on the mantel above the fire chimed the quarter.

He must be patient.

His instrument was ready, but would not be setting the great work in motion for several hours yet.

FORTY-FOUR

Heavitree Police Station. Later the same morning.

When her visitors from London had left, Cecilia sat for several minutes drumming her fingers on her desk. Then she reached into her handbag for her mobile phone and called Michael.

"Michael, you must be getting tired of the sound of my voice."

"I can't imagine that happening," he said. "What's up?"

"I've got something else to tell you that involves the academy. If you've got time. Actually, I'm afraid it also involves me."

"I've got time. Tell away."

"Do you know about the city banker who just got murdered, the one who got thrown through a window in Lombard Street?"

"Yes. I saw it on the news."

"Well, you see, I'm afraid that was my ex-husband."

"Oh Cecilia, how truly awful for you! I had no idea. I'm so sorry."

"Well, yes, it is awful—sort of weirdly awful. I mean, it's not quite the way you'd think. The fact is he'd dumped me a couple of years ago for someone else, and I was really miserable for a long time but honestly I've got over it and I've not thought about him now for months."

"*He* dumped *you*?"

"Afraid so."

"He must have been out of his mind."

In spite of herself, she smiled. It was nice that her friends were so loyal.

"That's sweet, Michael."

It was strange—or perhaps not so strange—that she'd never told Michael about her marriage break-up before. Anyway, she told it now, and went on tell him how she'd learned a few minutes ago that George had a connection—a *serious* connection— with the Academy for Philosophical Studies.

Michael whistled.

"Isn't it odd?" she said. "I don't hear anything about the academy for ages, and then suddenly it seems to be popping into my life everywhere I turn."

"It's odd. In fact it's more than odd. It's an extraordinary series of coincidences—almost as if you were being set up in opposition to the academy."

"I'm not sure I like that."

"I'm not sure I do."

The weight of it all struck her, and she fell silent for a moment. She thought of Hamlet: *There's a divinity that shapes our ends, rough hew them how we will.* Well, she supposed that was better than having no ends at all.

"Still, it's preferable to not having *any* purpose," Michael said.

"That's just *exactly* what I was thinking! Oh, Michael, thank you for being there and listening to all this."

When their conversation was over, Cecilia again sat for several minutes at her desk. But she no longer drummed her fingers on it. And she had a curious mixture of feelings.

She felt burdened by George's death and his connection with the academy.

But she also felt glad.

Why was she glad?

Well, for one thing Michael now knew about her failed marriage. And he knew about George.

So something good had come out of the morning.

And it was high time she did some work. She turned to her computer.

After some moments she stopped, and frowned.

Just why, exactly, was she glad that Michael now knew about her having been married?

Well, he was a friend, and a friend ought to know.

She shook her head.

No. That wasn't the reason. The real reason was, she was glad Michael now knew that she was, so to speak, secondhand.

Used.

"Pre-owned," that was the polite thing one said about used cars, wasn't it? "One previous owner."

So there were now no surprises about her for him to find out.

But that led to another question. Why should it matter? Why should she think Michael might care about her being previously married? Unless she thought… again she shook her head. That was ridiculous. Michael liked her, for sure. But he wouldn't be thinking of her like that.

She returned to the computer.

FORTY-FIVE

The Vicarage, St. Andrew's, Holborn Circus.

M ichael looked round the kitchen and nodded. The things that ought to be cooking were cooking. The things that were to be served cold were prepared. Wine was open and breathing. He'd just checked the table. For the moment there was nothing for him to do but wait until his guests arrived.

He would relax for a few moments — at which point, just as he was about to sit down, a thought came to him. Father Friedrich Spee, S.J. Whoever he was, perhaps he had written a book, got once into the news, done something that in the world's eyes would be of note? And if so, maybe there would be something about him on the internet?

It was a long shot, but it was surely worth a try.

He went up to his study, sat down at his computer, pulled up Safari, and began typing into the Google search box. He had hardly typed "Friedrich Spee v" and the search engine itself was suggesting a completion: "Friedrich Spee von Langenfeld."

He blinked with surprise. Naturally he'd been hoping to get lucky, but he'd hardly expected such a clear hit as this. He clicked on "search," and within seconds a slew of sites came up. Good Lord — how on earth was it that he'd never heard of a priest this well-known? He shrugged and clicked on a link at random.

A long article.

And now came his third surprise: he wasn't reading about a priest he might have met at Farm Street and then forgotten, *but about a priest who'd lived in the seventeenth century.*

He drew a sharp intake of breath.

Born at Kaiserswerth on the Rhine on February 25, 1591. Died at Trier, August 7, 1635. German Jesuit and poet, most noted as a critic of the trials for witchcraft.

With the article there was an image from a contemporary painting: and *yes!* — that could certainly fit the description that Cecilia had given him: dark hair and beard, dark eyes.

Michael sighed. Just what on earth was going on? Was someone playing a joke? Did the seventeenth century Spee have a twenty-first century namesake and double?

A chime from the front door — the first of his guests had arrived.

His questions would have to wait.

Forty-Six

Sherwood Road. Evening of the same day.

After supper James Hanlon told Alison that he was not to be disturbed, left her safely ensconced in front of the television, then went into his study, and locked the door. There as he had been instructed he opened the boxes and saw for the first time what they contained. In each, as if sleeping, lay a large ugly doll, the color of ash, dressed in a loose, drab coat.

He stared at them.

These were the instruments of the one they served? They were revolting. He'd seen better-looking corpses. He'd been with tramps that hadn't washed or had a change of clothes for months and smelt better.

For a moment he wondered whether what he was to do could possibly be right. He remembered the man in the Rolls, pulling at his hand with his cold skin and sniffing him and staring at him.

But then he remembered the promises.

He bit his lip, and looked again at the dolls.

For now they lay in their boxes, asleep. That had been for the journey from London. Now they must wake up. It was up to him to see that they did.

It was all just as the letter had told him it would be. In the corner of one of the boxes, resting in the straw, was a round jar. It contained an ointment whose smell was so sharp and pungent it seemed to burn his nostrils as he opened it. The ointment had to be smeared on each doll—on the stubby feet, the fingers with nails like claws, the big domed foreheads. It tingled unpleasantly on his fingers as he used it.

The job done, he stood back and waited.

A minute passed and nothing happened.

Had he left something out? Were they—?

One of them twitched. Then the other. Their eyes opened, watery and gray. Their mouths worked as if they were chewing. Suddenly they both sat up and looked at him. Moving, they were even uglier than before. Their stink filled the room.

He knew what he had to do next.

He lifted each from the table and set it on the ground, almost gagging as he did so. Suppressing his revulsion, he quickly led the creatures along the back passage, down the back stairs, and so to the back door that led to the vegetable garden.

He said nothing. They probably couldn't understand words and they surely couldn't speak. But they seemed to know what to do and followed him just as the man had promised.

They came to the back door. Feeling as if he were in a bad dream he opened it for them and the creatures waddled through. Without a backward look they continued on their way and into the gloom. He stood watching until there was no longer any sight of them.

The smell, mercifully, was beginning to fade, dissipating into the evening air, which was fresh and sweet.

Suddenly a brown hare with long black-tipped ears hopped onto the grassy bank beside the lettuces and sat there, less than two meters away from him. It wrinkled its nose. In the light from the door he could see everything about it: shiny eyes, whiskery face, brown fur. And it was big: surely not far off four kilos.

For several minutes the hare sat and looked at him. Something about the *way* it looked suggested it didn't think much of what it saw. Then it turned and lollopped majestically away, tail down, black dorsal clearly visible, across the lettuces towards the privet hedge and so to the dark farmland beyond.

Again, for a moment, Hanlon wondered. Did he really know what he was doing? What he *had* done?

He frowned and closed his eyes... then turned back to his study.

His hands were itching.

Sticky.

The ointment was still on them and it was starting to burn.

He went to the bathroom and ran water over them. He squeezed the liquid soap, then scrubbed his palms and fingers.

Better. That felt better. Cooling and sweet, the water was.

Yet... his hand wasn't clean. He scrubbed harder. Words were coming into his mind. Words from school. Words he didn't want to remember. But he couldn't stop them.

Here's the smell of blood still: all the perfumes of Arabia will not sweeten this little hand.

Now just what the hell had *that* got to do with anything?

FORTY-SEVEN

The Vicarage, St. Andrew's, Holborn Circus. The same evening.

"Bill," Michael said, pouring coffee when his guests had finished their dessert, "your period's the seventeenth century, isn't it?"

Bill Jardine grinned. "The seventeenth century, and whatever no one else in the department wants to teach that term."

"But wasn't your doctoral thesis on relationships between England and France under James?"

"Yes it was! A thesis that's mercifully never been published and with luck will remain buried in the oblivion it richly deserves, since I'm now convinced my main proposal was completely wrong."

"Oh! Well, anyway, in the course of your researches so richly deserving oblivion, did you ever hear of a Jesuit called Friedrich Spee?"

"Friedrich Spee von Langenfeld? Yes, I've heard of him. An interesting fellow, to say the least."

Michael set down the coffee pot.

"Has everyone got what they need? Good. Please, would you tell me about him?"

"Well, let's see… I don't know anything about his youth or childhood, but I do know that in 1627 the Bishop of Würzburg asked the Jesuits to send him a confessor for condemned witches, and the chap they chose was Spee, who spent the next two years trying to comfort people who were being sent to the stake for witchcraft—most of them women. One was a blind girl. There were a couple of children. From what Spee wrote later it's obvious he was present when some of them were being examined, and he was profoundly disturbed by it. He wrote, *Vidi lacrimas innocentium*: I've seen the tears of the innocent."

He'd seen things he'd rather not see—that's what Cecilia had said.

Bill Jardine stared at him for a moment, then continued, "In the end, Spee couldn't take it any more. The bishop's men and the city fathers began to bar him hearing confessions. They were afraid he'd take the victims' professions of innocence to higher authority. So he went away. But he wasn't finished. He wrote a book—*Cautio criminalis*, addressed to the magistrates of Germany—and he exposed the whole thing for what it was.

"He pointed out the lunacy of examination by torture. Either your victim confesses, in which case she's guilty, or she doesn't—in which case she must be in league with the devil to stand the pain. Spee was also, I think, the first person to point out that torture is actually useless as a way of getting reliable information, because most of the time the victim will say anything just to stop the pain. He said at one point the only reason why everyone in Germany didn't get condemned as a wizard was because everyone hadn't been tortured. And in any case, he insisted on grounds of mere human decency that no matter how terrible the crimes of which someone was accused, they still had a right to decent treatment, and that included having a lawyer present to act on their behalf."

Naomi chuckled. "I assume the last American Vice-President never read Spee, then?"

Only a few days earlier the former Vice-President had openly defended his administration's use of "enhanced interrogation"—a technique of questioning that most people regarded as indistinguishable from torture, and that the new administration had renounced.

"I'd rather not speculate about what that man reads," Bill said. "Anyway, Spee's book went through a lot of printings, and in the end it was a real factor in stopping the witch hunts. So he didn't live for nothing."

"He was something of a hero, then," Michael said.

"I think he was, though clearly he didn't think of himself that way. And I dare say he couldn't have acquired the knowledge he had to denounce the crime if he'd not had some part in it. I think he realized that. At any rate he never complained and he certainly didn't pose as a hero. But the fact remains, his book is in some ways a monument to human decency. He exposed and demolished every aspect of the trials — including all the private vendettas and financial corruption, not just the torture. I dare say it made him some powerful enemies."

"What happened to him?" Michael asked.

"I think he just went quietly on being a Jesuit. He wrote some rather beautiful poetry. And he died at Trier in 1635 helping plague victims. I suppose that was pretty heroic too."

FORTY-EIGHT

On the road towards R.A.F. Harlseden.

Whoever programmed the androids intended them to keep out of sight, at least for this stage of their operations. This was made easier tonight by the fact that southwest England was overcast anyway. The creatures moved discreetly along winding Devon roads, keeping to the deeper shadow of hedgerows and trees, avoiding curious eyes.

Their smell, however, could not be avoided.

A motorist with the driver's side window open saw nothing out of the ordinary in the headlights but found himself choking at the stench of rottenness that came to him out of the darkness—from a hedgerow at the side of the road, he rather thought.

But the car sped on past the smell, and the motorist had other things on his mind. Soon he forgot the brief unpleasantness.

In a house near the road a dog roused himself, scented for several seconds, then got up from his bed and barked furiously, his hackles raised.

"What is it, Joe?" his master said, looking up from his book.

Joe growled and pointed.

His master got up from his chair, went to the window, and peered out.

Meanwhile Joe, sensing that the danger had passed, gave a final growl, returned to his bed, and again settled himself into his favorite position.

A few minutes later he was asleep.

Thus unseen and largely unnoticed, the androids went their way. A sudden shower enveloped them in driving rain for several minutes, and then ceased as quickly as it had begun. The fact of it registered on their data banks but in no way altered their progress.

Droplets gleamed on the domed foreheads and splashed drab coats as the creatures waddled on towards their target.

FORTY-NINE

St. Andrew's Vicarage.

Michael Aarons was not an inhospitable man, but he was glad when his visitors went.

He needed to think.

He returned first to his computer.

He'd gathered from Bill as they were leaving that there'd recently been a complete translation into English of *Cautio criminalis*, published by the University of Virginia in 2003. He went to Amazon. Ah—there it was, in print and available. He ordered a copy.

Then he sat back in his chair and reflected.

Clarity, Michael, clarity.

Try not to leap to any conclusions.

What explanations are available?

Theory number one: someone claiming to be a seventeenth-century Jesuit was involving Cecilia in an elaborate hoax. True, the man didn't actually *claim* much of anything other than that his name was Friedrich Spee and that he was a Jesuit. But he had a great deal of good information about Cecilia and her family, about Michael, and about the academy. Where did he get it? Who was he really? And if it were a hoax, what was the point?

Theory number two: it wasn't a hoax. The seventeenth century Jesuit really did have a twenty-first century namesake and lookalike who was a member of the Society of Jesus, who had perhaps met Michael at Farm Street, and had gone to Exeter and talked to Cecilia. An odd story in itself, made odder by the fact that Michael had no recollection of ever having encountered such a man, and the Jesuits at Farm Street appeared to have no record of his ever having been there. Of course it was possible that the sister Michael talked to was lying. But why would she have lied?

Theory number three: Cecilia had been having hallucinations. But was she exhibiting hallucinatory behavior? Ridiculous. On the phone she was balanced, sane, and funny — just as she always was. In fact she was quite delightful. She laughed when he said John Thorpe was the perfect sleazy salesman. He loved the way she laughed. And then she always — for God's sake Michael! — he was supposed to be thinking about theories!

Theory number four? Cecilia was lying. Rubbish. He'd have staked his life on her truthfulness.

So much for naturalistic explanations. What of the supernatural, since he claimed to believe in it?

Theory number five, then. Cecilia was seeing some kind of ghost. A malevolent visitant? A demon? Saint Ignatius said to question oneself about the beginning, the middle, and the end of such incidents. All right. Whoever-or-whatever-it-was greeted her in the name of the Lord Jesus Christ, and had so far told her to pray, to think carefully, not to leap to conclusions, and to talk to her family and her friend Michael Aarons. Did that sound like the behavior of a malevolent visitant? Hardly. Remember also that Figaro seemed to like him: dogs were sometimes sensitive on such issues when humans were not.

Which led straight on to theory number six: Cecilia had been granted a true corporeal vision of the seventeenth-century Jesuit who wrote against torture. The sign that her vision was from God would be in the guidance toward sanctity that went with it: and such guidance did seem to have been part of her experience. He told her to pray, and to watch! This theory, if accepted, would of course carry with it one important consequence. It would require her to take what her visitor said *very* seriously.

So—what?

So Michael was going to telephone Cecilia and tell her he thought perhaps she was being visited by a departed saint?

If he were wrong, that would not be helpful.

If he were right, then she was in better hands than his.

He sighed.

The truth was, as a result of his evening at the computer and with his friends, he now had a great deal more information.

And as a result of *that*, he was more confused than ever.

FIFTY

The Cavalieres, the same evening.

The family had just got back from taking the dogs for their final walk of the day when Father Spee emerged from the darkness.

"Good evening," he said.

"Good evening, Father," Cecilia said. "Papa, Mama—this is Father Spee. I told you about him."

"I'm honored to meet you," Father Spee said. "Professor Cavaliere, your book *Rome and the Gods*—that is a magnificent piece of work."

"Thank you, Father," Papa said, plainly as surprised as he was pleased.

"And now," Father Spee said, "there is work for you, Cecilia Anna Maria, just as I said there would be. At Royal Air Force Harlsden."

"For me? What kind of work?"

"You must go there. Now. To the launch site at the Harlsden Royal Air Force base."

"That's a *missile* launching site, Father. Top secret. I don't think they take too kindly to unscheduled visitors."

"The powers of hell are at work there," he said. "They will destroy many and they will use the missiles to do it."

"Then wouldn't it be wiser to warn them at the base?" Papa said, "Shouldn't we telephone them?"

"We can telephone the Heavitree Road police station," Cecilia said, "and they'll liaise with the R.A.F. police."

"You can do that," Spee said, "but they will not be able to get through to the R.A.F. And then they will send patrol cars to the base and they will not be able to do anything. This is the work of the academy—the academy of which you three all know too well. It's because of that link that I am sent to you now—to *you*"—he looked directly at Andrea and Rosina—"and to your daughter."

"Well," Papa said, "I dare say we can try."

Spee smiled. "You aren't asked to be successful. You are merely asked to be faithful."

"There'll be Royal Air Force Police on duty at the gate," Cecilia said. "We certainly could go there and *tell* them we've been told there's a threat. That would make sense, wouldn't it?"

"Do you know the way?" Papa asked.

"I do," Cecilia said. "It'll take us about twenty minutes to get there."

"All right," Papa said. "The car's here, it's a nice night, and I guess"—looking to Cecilia—"*you'd* object if we were breaking any laws. So let's take a moonlight drive to R.A.F. Harlsden, and see what happens."

He threw her the keys, as he always did.

Again Spee smiled.

"Then, my children," he said, "we shall see what happens when God's servants move in the world. Go to the site. Go to the place where they will fire the missiles. And go with God."

He turned without another word and walked off down into the gloom under the trees. They watched him go for a few seconds, then could see only moonlit grass and darkness.

They looked at each other but for a moment nobody said anything, as if vanishing were simply Father Spee's way. Then—

"Come on," Mama said as soon as they'd put the dogs

into their respective houses. "If we're doing it, let's do it. I haven't sat in the back of a car with Papa in the moonlight for a long time."

"Now I get it," Cecilia said. "You two just want an opportunity to fool around."

She walked round to the driver's side of the car, got in, and inserted the key in the ignition.

"Just joking," Mama said, and got in beside her. "You get in the back, Papa."

"Yes dear."

It seemed they were going to R.A.F. Harlsden.

FIFTY-ONE

The first thing both of the R.A.F. policemen noticed was the smell.

"Jesus!" Sergeant Michael O'Reilly gagged as the stench hit the back of his mouth. Sickly-sweet and fetid, like unburied corpses. "For Christ's sake, will you look at that! What the hell *are* they?"

Retching and gagging, his colleague turned from the fence line and stared at the road. About twenty-five yards from the barricade, squat figures in drab coats were waddling out of the gloom toward them. Two of them, moving with an awkward, ugly gait that was as menacing as it was clumsy. The coats flapped, and even at this range the smell was appalling.

"Mother of God! Some kind of sick joke?"

"I'm reporting it. Check them out, Joe!"

Warrant Officer Joseph Black stepped out of the guard shack, SA80 assault rifle at the ready. Still coughing, O'Reilly tried to reach for the telephone—

His fingers refused to move. What was the matter with him? *His fingers wouldn't move.* His hand was dead. His arm was dead. He—

***

The barrier rose.

Silence, save for wind sighing in the trees.

The two androids waddled past rigid figures and useless weapons, on toward the base.

Fifty-Two

It took Cecilia and her parents about twenty minutes to reach the turning into the missile site. Papa's Subaru Outback handled well on the unmade road, and at first they scarcely slowed. Soon, however, rain began to spot the windshield. The rain grew heavier and she eased back on the accelerator. Within minutes they were driving through a downpour. Puddles and damp stones gleamed in the headlights, and the wipers could scarcely cope.

Rounding a curve in the road, they saw lights through the driving rain. Cecilia eased back the accelerator even further.

"Here, I think, is the end of the ride. Wait a minute, though — it's open. That's odd."

They were now close enough to see the barricade, and they could all see that it was raised. They could also see two uniformed men. One was inside the hut beside the barricade. The other was standing outside in the rain, his weapon pointing toward them.

"*Damn!*" Cecilia braked hard, bringing the Subaru to an abrupt halt that threw them forward in their seat-belts. "Were they *expecting* us?"

The rain eased up and then stopped even more abruptly than it had begun. But the muzzle that was pointed at them did not waver.

"Look," Cecilia said with a coolness she didn't feel, "I don't know what's going on, but that Air Force policeman who's covering us with an SA80 is making me *very* nervous. I hope he isn't nervous too, but in case he is, we'd better do this by the book."

The others nodded.

Cecilia reached forward and switched off the headlights and the windshield wipers, being careful to leave on the parking lights. She lowered her window, not for a moment taking her eyes off the scene at the guard shack, and taking care even at this distance to avoid any sudden movement. Then she reached into the pocket of her jeans for the wallet containing her warrant card. She passed it to Mama.

"Would you mind holding this?" she said. "I'm not sure whether we're in trouble or not, but if we are it just might help get us out of it. Mama, please put both your hands on top of the dashboard, where he can see them, holding the wallet open so he can see my warrant card. When we move forward, whatever you do, don't drop your hands out of his line of sight. And Papa, please, put your hands on your head. Where he can see them. I'm serious."

"I know," Papa said, and did as she asked.

Finally, keeping her own hands clamped on top of the wheel where they were plainly visible, she inched the Subaru forward into the pool of light that surrounded the guard shack.

The security policeman was still looking down the road, to a point now several yards behind them. His companion inside the guard shack did not move.

"What on earth's the *matter* with them?" Mama said.

"I haven't the slightest idea," Cecilia said.

FIFTY-THREE

After another moment, as by unspoken agreement, the three of them got out of the Subaru and walked over to the motionless policeman. Standing well clear of the muzzle of the SA80, Cecilia gave the man's arm a gentle tap. Nothing. She might as well have been tapping a tailor's dummy.

Papa shook his head. "This is weird."

Cecilia grimaced.

"What on earth's that ghastly smell?" Mama said.

Cecilia shook her head. The air was generally fresh after the downpour, but around the barrier there was an undertone of something else, something sickly sweet and vile.

She walked with Mama toward the hut. Papa, after a moment's further examination of the motionless security man, followed them.

The man inside the hut was frozen in the act of reaching for the phone. Cecilia went in and picked it up herself, brushing against his motionless hand —

It felt stiff, like a piece of furniture. But it was *not* a piece of furniture. It was a man. Warm. Alive. But locked up. Rigid. Like a tailor's dummy. It was horrible.

"Well?" It was Mama, standing at the doorway and peering in. Cecilia tried the phone.

"It's dead."

She took her mobile out of her jeans and tried it. It too was dead. And she had only just recharged it. Papa tried his. The same.

"Mine's in the car," Mama said, "but it looks as if something's messing them up, doesn't it?"

Of course Mama's didn't work either.

"Damn," Cecilia said. "I've made a bad mistake. I thought I'd wait and communicate with the station if there actually seemed to be something to report. I was probably more concerned about not looking a fool than about operational sense. But now there *is* something to report, and I can't communicate. Is the car dead too?"

Without a word Papa got in and turned the ignition. The engine started.

"Well," he said, "at least we've still got transport."

Cecilia looked round at her parents. "So now we've two choices: go back and get help, in which case we might be too late if there's something happening here that we should try to stop, or go on, in which case we might get ourselves killed. Suggestions? Recommendations? Something I haven't thought of?"

"I was doubtful before we started," Mama said. "But we can't go back now. Not when what Father Spee said is starting to make sense." She gestured at the motionless figures. "Just look at them! We've got to go on."

Cecilia nodded, then pointed to the board.

"'Use of deadly force authorized.' You know what that means, don't you?"

"Yes," Mama said, "it's government-ese for 'We shoot trespassers'."

"Could terrorists fire the missiles?" Papa said.

Cecilia thought for few seconds before answering. "Up to a few minutes ago I'd have said, no, certainly not. There's no way anyone rogue can fire those missiles. There are too many safeguards. But now?" She glanced past her parents at the frozen figures. "If it's terrorists, how on earth did they manage *this*? And if they're able to manage this, what else can they manage?"

"Your friend Father Spee did say, 'Go to the site. Where they fire the missiles.' I remember that clearly," Mama looked at Papa, who nodded. "And he seems to have known what he was talking about. So maybe we should go there. To the site. After all, this is only the gate."

"You're right," Papa said, "And if it wasn't for Spee, we wouldn't know about this at all. I've no idea what's going on, but it looks as if we probably ought to do what he said."

Cecilia looked at them, and hesitated. She knew they were right—she must go on. But she, after all, was a professional. They weren't.

"I should go on," she said. "That would be best. You two go back and get help."

"Right," Papa said. "Of course we're going to leave you here. Get in, both of you. We're wasting time."

Still she hesitated. Although the rain had stopped, the air was still damp.

"We're not going back," Mama said, getting into the back seat. "So either you can walk on by yourself and we'll just follow you, or you could be sensible and get in. You'll get there a lot quicker if you do."

"And that could be important," Papa said.

That was the clincher. She got in beside Papa.

"I think you're both wonderful," she said.

"Yes," Papa said as he released the parking brake. "Wonderfully crazy. And there's always the chance we might *not* get shot. We might get lucky and just end up in jail."

Mama giggled. "Yes," she said, "that's right. Thirty years with time off for good behavior ought to cover it."

Papa guffawed.

Not for the first time, it occurred to Cecilia that her parents were delinquent.

FIFTY-FOUR

R.A.F. Harlsden. A few minutes later.

Up the road the androids advanced, waddling side by side. A mile or so past the guard post, where the road divided, the androids also parted company. One went left to Alfa-1, one went right to Alfa-2.

Yet their processes were still linked. Simultaneously—in fact, at the exact same moment—they approached the entrances to the two control centers. Simultaneously the occupying security police were assaulted by stench and paralyzed. Simultaneously the androids lay hands on them and waited until, mouths working as by remote control, the still unconscious men uttered the codes that gave admission to the control centers. Simultaneously the androids left them—still frozen, their weapons in their hands, unused and useless.

Simultaneously, claw-like fingers punched in the codes.

Now only minutes behind the androids, the Subaru swished up the road, headlights blazing. Mama, uncharacteristically melodramatic, had suggested they put the lights out and approach whatever they were approaching cautiously.

"I don't think so," Papa said. "First, with lights dimmed we'd look sinister. Possibly dangerous. People shoot people who look dangerous. With lights on, we look like what we are: a trio of idiots. People don't always bother to shoot idiots. Second — or is it third? — if we put out the lights, I can't actually see where this thing's going and we'll probably drive into a tree and break our necks. Which might impair our ability to save the world for democracy. That *is* what we're doing, isn't it?"

Cecilia grinned. "Probably," she said.

After a few minutes they came to a fork in the road. Papa slowed.

"Do you know which way?"

"They both lead to missile sites," Cecilia said. "Take either. So far as I know, it makes no difference."

Papa shrugged, and went right.

FIFTY-FIVE

R.A.F. Harlsden. The Launch Control Capsule
of Control Center Alfa-2.

L ance and David looked up in surprise as a warning buzz
announced that the correct four-digit code had been entered
from outside, and the capsule door was about to open.

"Unannounced inspection," David muttered. "They're
making sure we aren't asleep. Or entertaining women. Ten dollars says it's security."

But Lance wasn't so sure.

"Wait a minute," he said. "I think there's something wrong.
That's not security."

Both men got to their feet. The door opened and something
like a hideous doll waddled in. For one sickening instant Lance
registered it, appalled. It was vile. Not merely vile smelling and
vile in appearance, but worse, vilely insinuating, sliding into
his mind even as its stench slid into his mouth and lungs, defiling him, defiling his thoughts.

So what was all that stuff the family had brainwashed him with
about duty and honor? Surely a good way to keep him docile. To make
sure he never did anything HE wanted...

And Sophie, who knew what she was up to when he wasn't around?
Hadn't he noticed her eyeing the director of the orchestra? Flashing
him that come-hither smile —

NO!

He wasn't having it. Sophie was everything that was good and sweet. His family was good. Gritting his teeth he defied the insinuating thoughts.

The android snarled.

For something like a minute Lance struggled for control of his own mind. Again the creature snarled, bending more and more power on him. He felt powerless. Held.

And then suddenly he saw. The creature was right!

And he heard. Well, perhaps he did not exactly *hear*: the voice was in his head, rather than the air, but it was clear, nonetheless, telling him things he'd surely have known if he hadn't been such a child.

Everything is vile. There is no point in resisting in order to preserve a world that deserves to die. It would be better to help. It would be better to cleanse it.

Ah, now he understood.

The creature was laying its hands on the console, as of course it should. Wise creature! Clever hands engaging the module, clever eyes flickering over hidden circuitry, extracting, deciphering!

And now the voice was telling him, him and David, telling them what they needed to know. Numbers. A sequence.

The enable code.

It would launch the missiles.

What a clever creature it was! A wise creature! And of course it was right. The world needed to be cleansed. The missiles would do it. The missiles should be fired.

He dialed the code into the console.

David was doing the same.

But what of Alfa-1? What were they doing in Alfa-1? If they did not act there too, then nothing would come of it.

The answer came at once. The speakers warbled. Isabella was as cool as ever.

Enable Code received… Confirming… Enable code accepted. Warning. Missiles arming… Confirmed.

Warning. Missiles armed and ready to launch.

Launch vote required within one hundred and twenty seconds.

Use your key, said the voice in his head. *Give the launch vote.*

He reached for his key. David was reaching for his.

And counting, Isabella said.

One hundred and twenty… One hundred and nineteen…

But then, just as he moved to obey, there came to him another voice, a different voice.

Lance, it said, *just what the hell do you think you're doing?*

He didn't like this voice nearly so much—not at first. It was abrupt, peremptory. Yet there was something familiar about it. He'd known it from childhood. Yes, it was sometimes abrupt and peremptory with him, just as it was now. But it was mostly merry and kind. And it had never led him astray yet.

Use your key, the first voice said. It was strong and seductive. It was clever, intelligent, and wise. Surely he should do what it said?

But the new voice was strong, too. *Lance, I thought you said there was a chain of command?*

Sudden tears started into his eyes. Honest, wholesome tears. He *did* know that voice. And he loved it.

Son, didn't you say lawful authority's what distinguishes a real military from a rabble? Isn't that what you told Sophie? Isn't that what you believe? So whose orders are you taking?

Abruptly, Lance lowered the key and turned to the android.

"Excuse me," he said, "but who the hell are you? And just where do you come in the chain of command?"

FIFTY-SIX

Papa brought the Subaru to a halt at the entrance to the control center compound, directly opposite the guard shack. There was the same sickening smell. It was obvious at once that here too the occupants were paralyzed.

The three of the them got out as a figure emerged from the shadows.

It was Spee.

"How on earth did you get here?" Cecilia said.

"All times and places are in the hand of our Beloved," he said. "Or if the language of science pleases you more you could put it in another way, and say it's a matter of time and relative dimensions in space."

"*What?*" Cecilia said.

"Going faster than light, even maybe some kind of time travel," Papa said, surprising her. "One of our science buffs was telling me about it the other day. I gather some people think it's theoretically possible. The problem is, they also think you'd need the energy of an exploding star to do it. So it's not too practical for us just at present."

"Exactly," Spee said, "not too practical for *you*! But to our Beloved the power of a star, the power of a galaxy, are *quasi stilla situllae*, as a drop in a bucket." He turned to Cecilia. "So now are you ready?"

"What must I do?"

"The control center," he said. "It will be dangerous for you."

"Show me."

"I will," he said. "But first I must be sure you understand. What you are about to do is dangerous—to you personally. Even if you succeed, *you may die*. You are hazarding your life. Do you understand?"

She nodded.

She ran to Papa, then to Mama, and hugged and kissed them both. Papa said nothing, just held her tight for a moment, then whispered, "God bless you."

"Do what you have to do, *bella*," Mama whispered. "Take care. No, that's not what you're going to do, is it? Well, whatever. God bless you."

"Thank you," Cecilia said. She turned back to Spee. "I'm ready," she said.

"Very well," he said, "come."

"What can we do?" Papa asked.

"Pray," Spee said. "Make yourselves channels to your daughter of our Beloved's presence and power. That is all any of us can do. Now go home. I promise you it will be best. And I promise you I will bring her to you if I can."

Papa looked at him quizzically for a moment, then nodded.

"All right," he said.

Cecilia and Spee walked on.

"I wish I could speak to Michael," she said suddenly.

"Why?"

"I'd—I'd like to ask him to pray for me."

He looked at her, and shook his head. "And you say you are 'not much of a believer.' Give me your mobile telephone."

"I'm afraid it's not working."

"Please."

She produced it and handed it to him. He did something

to it—she did not see what—and handed it back. It was obviously on.

"What—?"

He smiled. "Call it a free upgrade," he said. "It'll work for you to call your friend. But be quick!"

He walked on.

She got through at once.

"Hello," Michael said. "St. Alban's—"

"Michael, it's me. I've no time to talk. But I've got to do something rather dangerous. Well, *really* dangerous. Will you think about me—*pray* for me, please?"

"Of course I will." His words were calm, but she could tell from his voice that he was not.

"Oh, thank you, Michael. And Michael, I—I—I've got to go."

"I understand. *Please* be careful."

"I've tried that. It's boring."

Her weak little joke seemed to work. She sensed his smile, and when he spoke again his voice was not so tense: "Then go with God."

"You too, Michael."

She caught up with Spee, who'd already passed the gate.

"By the way," he said as they walked on, as if something had just occurred to him, "that's another reason why you're better qualified for this task than you think."

"What's that?"

"You're in love."

"Michael's a priest, and I asked him to pray for me."

"So he is and so you did," Spee said. But he was smiling.

They had reached the control center.

Cecilia did not see what Spee did to operate the lift, but with an unpleasant hiss the doors slid apart.

The cavernous steel box gaped before her.

But then there was a mild commotion in the darkness to her left.

Leaves and grass rustled...

And out the darkness scampered something black and hairy that shot past her into the lift, then turned and looked at her, feathery tail waving

"*Figaro*! How on earth did you get here?"

"Figaro, my small friend, how good to see you!" Spee seemed not at all surprised. "And you have arrived at just the right moment."

Figaro wagged his tail furiously.

"But I put him in the house. I know I did!"

Spee smiled.

"Yes, you did. And yet here he is. And now he will go with you. There's more to that dog than you might think."

"I'm beginning to realize there's more to everything than I might think."

"Exactly. There always is. Now go, child, and hinder those who would unlock chaos."

A moment later she was stepping into the lift.

FIFTY-SEVEN

Saint Andrew's, Holborn Circus.

The interior of the Lady Chapel at Saint Andrew's is warm and comforting. But on this occasion Michael was not comforted.

Where was Cecilia? She'd said she had to do something dangerous. *Really dangerous* — her exact words.

Dangerous enough for her to phone him and ask his prayers?

He had no idea what that could be, but... it must be bad. Of course he was glad she'd phoned him — but he may as well face it, he was also terrified. She would do whatever she considered to be her duty, of that he was sure. And God forbid she should not. But still he found himself sweating at the mere thought of what might happen to her.

Was Father Spee with her? He wished he'd asked. The fact was, once she'd said she was in danger every other thought had gone out of his head.

He shook his head. She'd given him a job to do and he'd said he'd do it — as she, no doubt, she was doing hers.

She'd relied on him.

So — it was time to act. It was time to show whether there was anything to him or whether he was all just talk.

Do it for her.

Calmly as he could, he began to pray.

Gently, persistently, he brought her name before the One Name, the One Who loved her more even than he did, yet would consent to use him as a channel to her of grace.

For her Lord, as you know her needs. Do, or do not do, as she needs.

FIFTY-EIGHT

R.A.F. Harlsden.

Use *the key!*, said the voice in Lance's head again. But it had changed its tone. Perhaps frustration triggered in it something akin to anger. Whatever the reason, the voice was no longer wise and seductive. It was cold and cruel, threatening him with instant death if he did not obey.

And there surely it — or the one who programmed it — made a mistake, at least as regards Lancelot Scott. The claim to greater wisdom could perhaps still have seduced him, for he was a young man who had no high view of his own wisdom. But the threat of death? Lancelot Scott had sworn to defend the constitution and laws of the United States, laying down his life if necessary. He would fulfill those oaths.

Use the key or die! the creature demanded yet again.

"I think not," he said. "You have no lawful authority here. Get out."

And now something else sprang to life in him. The spirit perhaps that had burned in his grandfather on that day, legendary in the annals of R.A.F. 71 Squadron, when in his lone Spitfire he took on a mass of Stukas and downed three of them by the time the rest of the squadron came up.

In that spirit, or something like it, Lancelot Scott now did the last thing that the creature itself or the one who programmed it could have expected of a lone man faced with death at the hands of an adversary far stronger than he.

He attacked it.

And for precious seconds he fought it, toe to toe, while Isabella continued counting. *Seventy-one... seventy... sixty-nine...*

The match wasn't quite as uneven as one might have thought. The creature—though far stronger than it looked, far stronger than Lance—was not built for agility. And Lance, as he soon realized, was much faster on his feet.

He dodged in and out, avoiding its flailing blows and dancing round it, driving in short jabs of his own that probably did not hurt it but seemed at least momentarily to disorient it.

So he kept at it. Dodge and counterpunch. Dodge and counterpunch.

Dodge! Jab!

Duck! Jab!

Duck! Dodge! Jab! Jab!

This was not getting him anywhere. *Damn!*

In his frustration he plunged at the creature with renewed fury, driving in a hail of blows that actually knocked it back a foot or so.

And the seconds were passing.

The android snarled.

It did not exactly think, for it did not exist in the way that thinking—sweet, rational thought, a divine gift!—requires. But there was a kind of interaction between its neural pathways as the robotics expert had implanted them and the dark pseudo consciousness that had been imposed upon it by its maker. And by that interaction the android sensed in its own way that it could not control this particular human being to do its master's will.

There were qualities here that for some reason resisted the programming.

And time was being lost.

But there were other ways to achieve what was necessary. Let the human simply lose consciousness. Then the key of destruction could be taken from him and the work done anyway.

But it must happen quickly. The human at the other side of the capsule was already held fast and in position. And in the other capsule his fellow had already overcome the crewmembers there and was waiting.

Only this fool barred the way.

So the android was obliged to stand still, to restrain the instilled malice that drove it to strike at the man who defied it, and instead to bend all the power of its will simply to cause him to sleep. Nothing more.

Lance's arms were suddenly leaden. His eyelids drooped. Somewhere in the background he could hear Isabella still warbling her numbers... but he'd lost count of them. And he felt they were important... but he couldn't remember why.

"God help me," he said. Then felt himself stumble, and fall.

The android was looming over him, clawed fingers poised.

He struggled to move, to rise.

He couldn't.

He felt it take the launch key. He was sure this was not good.

Blackness.

FIFTY-NINE

The elevator.

The lift stopped. The doors slid open. Cecilia peered cautiously around. The smell was, if anything, stronger. Was this the underworld — *la città dolente*? Whatever it was, there was only one way to go. She emerged into a green-painted corridor and walked slowly down it toward a door, which was ajar, Figaro trotting beside her. She could hear a woman's voice over loud speakers. Cool. Impersonal. It was counting backward.

Do they always count backward in hell?

Perhaps they do everything backward in hell.

At the door she paused for a moment. Figaro waited beside her.

Then she stepped inside.

The stench that greeted her was revolting, and for a moment she simply could not comprehend the scene before her — a jumble of green consoles and tiny lights, here a half-empty coffee cup, there an open paperback novel, and opposite her a man in uniform coveralls, a key in his hand, standing by a console, motionless, as if paralyzed in the act of reaching towards it. And over all the voice continued, counting backward, disembodied, electronic, and implacable. *Forty-nine... forty-eight...*

Then she focused, suddenly aware of the foul thing in the far end of the chamber, appalling her with its smell, and even more, now she looked properly at it, with the malevolence of its gaze as it stared and snarled at a second man, also in coveralls, slumped motionless on the floor. As she watched, the foul thing bent over him and took something from him. It straightened up, its prize in its hand. Another key.

It turned towards a second console.

Another key.

Keys.

They will unlock chaos, Father Spee had said.

On the instant she saw.

"*NO!*" she cried.

It was just one word, but it was passionate, and it was as loud as she could make it. The creature turned back from the console and looked at her, its half-open mouth showing sharp, uneven teeth.

Cecilia felt at once the paralyzing pressure of its will, reaching into her mind and corrupting her thoughts, twisting everything she knew, everything it touched. Almost she succumbed.

But not quite.

Perhaps because, for all her uncertainty as to her faith, she had nonetheless come in deliberate service of the Love which she made no claim to understand, perhaps because she knew that Michael was praying for her and that Mama and Papa were bringing her before Love in their own ways, perhaps simply because she was not so alone in the capsule as she thought — perhaps for all of these reasons, where others had failed, Cecilia Cavaliere was able to resist.

The backward counting continued. *Thirty-nine... thirty-eight... thirty-seven...* The man nearest her had begun to move, key in hand, towards the console. She saw his name tag — his name was David, David Levi.

"No, David!" she cried again. "No, you must not!"

He didn't stop.

Cecilia went for him.

She seized his arm, and as he tried to shake her off she guided his own force and weight against him.

He was considerably heavier than she and surely as well-trained in unarmed combat. But she, though under assault, was still her own woman, and he, under alien control, was no match for her speed and delicacy. The key spun from his fingers, his feet went out from under him, and he crashed to the floor.

The android registered the continuing defiance of the one who had just entered the capsule, and stopped. Its information banks had absorbed what had happened with the other, the one who had first defied and assailed it, and now recognized similar qualities here. And there was an additional factor: this one was not part of the plan. It was not supposed to be here at all. The creature stood still: for the tiniest fraction of a millisecond the new information remained unabsorbed, and binary uncertainty threatened. But the programming was adequate, and there was no glitch. A decision was made. This one, too — this intruder — would be put to sleep.

Waves of tiredness swept through Cecilia. More than anything she wanted to lean against something, or better still to lie down. Her eyelids were like lead, her mind turning to mush.

The man she had just floored, the man called David, had meanwhile come to his knees and was fumbling for the key. He had it almost at once and got slowly to his feet, his eyes still fixed upon the console.

She clenched her fists, driving her nails so hard into her palms that they nearly cut into the flesh. She focused on the patches on his shirt, the movement of his hands — anything to avoid or overcome her desperate desire to sleep.

For the moment, she succeeded. She managed to back herself

against the console's bulk. There she faced David Levi and barred his way.

The backward counting continued.

Again the man called David shuffled forward, and this time he struck at her, a crude sideways blow as if to knock her from his path. Her movements were limited by her determination to block his way to the console, and so the blow caught her with full force on the arm, stinging and bruising her.

At which point Figaro, enraged that someone had struck his Cecilia, growled furiously and flung himself at her assailant's leg, closing sharp teeth on trouser and ankle, then hanging on for dear life.

David staggered, the pain penetrating even his drained and muddled consciousness, causing him to hesitate and look down.

The android snarled, again baffled.

And here was evidence of another mistake.

Those who created and programmed it scorned loyalty and regarded beasts as either fodder to be farmed or else an impediment to good hygiene. It would therefore never even have occurred to them to program their creature to control the devotion of an angry dog.

As for Cecilia, the sharp stab of pain in her arm when the blow struck her actually helped. It cleared her mind. And in her adversary's sudden distraction by Figaro she saw her chance. Summoning up her final reserves of strength, she sprang towards him from the console, ducked under his arm, whisked the key from his grip, and sent it spinning into the far reaches of the chamber.

But the effort had been her last. The android's numbing power continued to creep into her mind, sapping her energies. Exhausted and drained by it, she sank to her knees.

Oh dear God, I've had it.

She crumpled onto her side and lay still, unable to move.

She could hear the creature snarling. She sensed it advancing on her. She'd seen those clawed, crooked fingers that would surely tear her.

Figaro was still growling.

She wondered if dying would hurt.

She hoped the dean in the cathedral had been right. About the resurrection and eternal life and such. She hoped Michael was right about all manner of things being well.

There was a time when she'd nearly kissed him.

She wished she had, now.

SIXTY

The capsule.

The android was powerful, but its power was by no means unlimited. Distracted by its need to control Cecilia, it had weakened its hold on Lance Scott. And that, with such a spirit as his, it could not afford to do.

So Lance's mind had cleared a few seconds earlier—in time for him to see a black, hairy dog hanging on to David's leg, and then a woman with long dark hair using the opportunity to snatch the other key from David's hand and throw it into the corner of the capsule. Then she stumbled and sank to her knees, overcome just as he had been himself.

And the creature he'd fought, whatever it was, was now advancing on her.

He had no idea what was happening, what the creature was, or how or why they all came to be there.

But there's a fight going on and at least I'm damn sure whose side I'm NOT on!—with which thought he pulled himself jerkily to his feet, seized one of the metal chairs, and pitching himself forward as the creature bent to tear at the woman, shouted "No you don't!" and at the same time smashed the chair across its back.

The blow clearly registered, for the creature staggered.
Then it turned towards him.

But again — perhaps thanks to Lance's blow with the chair —
the android's hold had been weakened, this time its hold on
Cecilia.

She blinked. She heard Figaro growling.

She saw the creature in the corner of the chamber, snarling.

Then she saw the airman, a metal chair in his hands, standing
before it, defying it. She grinned — it was the man from Exeter,
the man with the MG. She staggered to her feet, grabbed the
other chair, and came to his side, facing the creature.

It hesitated for several seconds looking from one to the other,
seeming for the first time unable to focus its powers of control.

The airman glanced sideways at her — and smiled.

"You again!" he said. "Police lady!"

"Looks like it," she said. "Captain Scott, I believe?"

He nodded — then, as one who accepts the inexplicable
because there is no time for anything else —

"When it attacks," he said, "I think it's best if we keep moving
on either side of it — go for it from opposite ends. It's damn
strong — for God's sake keep out of its reach! But it's slow. And
I think it's possible to confuse it."

"Right!" She stepped away from him to her left as he suggested, now moving lightly on her feet, and feeling as she did
so a fierce, bright exhilaration. Positioned to her satisfaction,
she flashed a smile at her companion in arms and he grinned
back at her. For that instant she loved him.

"Do you think we can take it?" she said.

"Probably not."

She laughed. Perhaps it wasn't for nothing she was of the
same seed as those Cavalieres who were in the death-or-glory

charges at Grenoble and Pastrengo, or that young Andrea who had died at Rome defending the Italian flag.

She tossed her hair back and faced the creature.

"All right," she said softly, "let's see what you've got."

The attack when it came was faster than they might have expected. The creature seemed to have given up trying to control their minds — perhaps two such was more than it had been programmed for. But it was strong and it was vicious. It shot out arms that were surprisingly long and smashed blows at them both simultaneously. One struck Cecilia's legs and she staggered backwards, almost losing her balance.

She was vaguely aware that the same thing had happened to the airman.

There was a moment of confusion.

She recovered her balance, and faced the creature again.

Again it charged, its arms and fists swinging like pistons, but this time she was ready: she jumped clear and as she jumped slammed the chair at those flailing arms with all the force she could muster. There was a savage jolt and she heard herself gasp as the blow went home. The chair was almost twisted from her hands, but somehow she managed to hang on to it and keep her balance. She'd sensed the airman striking at it from the other side. And now they were at it in earnest, crashing around the capsule, the creature swinging and striking at them as they dodged and twisted, striking back as best they could.

This time it was the creature that staggered back a pace, and now stopped.

For a moment the three stood at an impasse, the two humans panting.

"How do you think we're doing?" Cecilia muttered, without taking her eyes off the creature.

"About as well as I expected."

"That bad!"

She sensed rather than heard his chuckle.

The voice over the speakers continued, implacable as ever.

Three... two... One... Zero.

A brief pause. Then—

Launch sequence aborted. Launch sequence aborted.

She took a firmer grip on her chair, feeling its balance, sensing how she might use it in the next attack.

It never came.

Instead, the creature emitted a snarl that sounded almost like frustration, then turned and left, leaving behind an open capsule door, an unpleasant memory, and a mercifully fading stench.

Sixty-One

The same, a few minutes later.

Figaro stopped growling.

Silence.

Slowly, cautiously, Cecilia relaxed, still breathing quickly, still watching the door.

The creature did not return. After another minute she sighed and put the chair down. Figaro shoved his head against her hand, so naturally she scratched it.

Then she turned to her companion in arms. For a moment they surveyed each other in silence.

"Hello again Captain Scott," she said. "That was easier than I expected."

He lowered his own chair and shook his head.

"What *was* it?" he said.

"I'm not sure," she said. "But nothing good."

"Well ma'am, I sure appreciate your help. And I know you're with the police. But you still have the advantage of me. And how on earth did you get in here?"

Cecilia smiled. "I'm Detective Inspector Cavaliere, Exeter CID. But as for how I got here—that's a long story and I'm not sure I know how to tell it. Let's just say you had a fight on your hands, and I was able to give a hand."

"And so you did."

She turned to see Father Spee standing in the doorway. "Actually, you gave each other a hand. You were both quite magnificent."

He walked in, smiling.

Scott looked confused as well he might.

"Your base was under attack, Captain Scott. Those creatures — you only saw one of them, but there are two — they had succeeded in controlling everything: the secret codes to enter this place, your guards, everyone, just as they controlled this good fellow." He nodded toward the second controller, who was still motionless. "And they would have fired the missiles. They would have made *you* fire the missiles. They had control of the other capsule, the codes were programmed in, and everything was ready. Except that you, Lancelot Scott, defied them."

"Me? Was I the only one? Why me?"

"That's a mystery, and only God knows the answer to it. But I can tell you this — your grandfather is proud of you. You delayed things until Cecilia Anna Maria arrived, and then the two of you delayed things still further. So the launch sequence was aborted. As soon as that happened, the creature's work had failed, and it withdrew. It was programmed for one thing. It knew no alternative. Between the pair of you, you defeated it. Or more importantly, you defeated the one who sent it."

"Us and Figaro," Cecilia said. "If hadn't been for Figaro, I'm not sure I could have done my bit. In fact I'm sure I couldn't."

"You're quite right!" Spee said. "It was the two of you and Figaro, my small and valiant friend."

Figaro thumped his tail enthusiastically. Spee bent down and scratched his head.

"So," he said, "*diligentibus Deum omnia cooperantur in bonum — to them that love God, all things work together unto good.*"

"And so what now?" Scott said. "I believe you. Given what's

happened, I don't see how I can do anything else. But what will happen now? You two are going to have to explain all this to a lot of people besides me."

"Actually, we aren't. And this is going to be a burden for you, after what you've just experienced. But what will happen now is that nothing will happen. Or at least, little of significance. And under the circumstances, given what *might* have happened, that's the best thing there could be."

"Nothing? But David here, all those others on the base — will they recover? Will they be all right?"

"They will recover." Spee went up to the one Cecilia had fought, peered into his eyes, and then nodded again. "He's a good young man. He'll take no harm." He turned back to the other two. "When we leave, they will all recover — your friend David here, the security guards, all of them — they will recover but they will remember nothing. Odd things about the evening will puzzle them — someone will wonder why he didn't notice the time passing, someone else will wonder why he's not standing where he thought he was, your friend David will probably wonder why his ankle is sore (Figaro's grip is not to be taken lightly), and because of what the screens and data banks will tell them, a lot of people will wonder if something has gone wrong with the equipment. But in the end they will decide that 'there must be a perfectly rational explanation' for all these things, even though they can't think what it is. And in a sense, of course, they will be right."

"So we're all just going to forget that any of this ever happened?"

"Not exactly 'we', Lancelot. You see, that's *your* burden. They will forget. But *you* fought the creature. You defied it. Its being is burned into your memory. And I can't remove that, for it's a part of you. In a way, it's now who you are. You'll have to live with what you've seen, and you must be content simply to know you did well and that the angels know your courage. You won't be able to tell the story of what you just did because no one will believe you. And no one will believe you because no one will want to believe you."

Scott nodded slowly. "I see, or at least I think I do. Well, I guess that's okay. I still think I'd rather know than not know."

"I rather thought you would," Spee said. He pointed to the keys, both now on the floor.

"Can you replace those?" he said. "It will be one less thing for them to explain."

Lance did as he asked.

"I've replaced the seals as well as I can, but someone will surely notice that they're cracked," he said.

Spee nodded, stepped over to them, and for a moment or so Cecilia was not sure what he was doing: but when he stepped back, the cracks had disappeared.

Scott stared at him. "How on earth did you do that?"

Spee smiled. "A tiny adjustment of matter in space," he said. "The technique's a little advanced for the early twenty-first century, but no law has been broken. Is there anything else?"

Lance looked around. He picked up a book and straightened the chairs. He surveyed the capsule again, and then shrugged.

"It's looking pretty well the way it always looks," he said.

Spee nodded.

"Good," he said. "Then Cecilia Anna Maria and I must go." He smiled again. "But first, Lancelot, to accompany your burden and in time, I think, to lighten it—or at least, to provide you with a new and more interesting burden—I offer you a gift. *Try the rose garden.* Your friend Sophia. Marry her if she will have you. I think she will. You love each other and with patience you can give each other and the world much. But first seek wise counsel. Together. It won't be easy for either of you."

Cecilia stared in surprise.

"And now come," he said to her. "You and I are not finished. We have more to do."

"What about Figaro?" she said, looking round. Figaro was nowhere to be seen.

He smiled. "Figaro will get safely home, I promise. Now, will you trust me?"

"Yes. Just a minute, though."

She turned back to Scott.

"Goodbye, Captain Scott. It was nice seeing you again. I hope you got that battery connection fixed on the MG."

"Yes ma'am, I did. And the engine cleaned, oil change, everything. It's running beautifully. I always pay careful attention to advice from beautiful women who rescue me!"

"Do you?" she said, feeling slightly light-headed. "Well then here's a bit more. If I were you I'd get rid of that seersucker jacket. It makes you look a bit of a prat, actually. You look much nicer in coveralls. And I bet you look great in uniform."

"Goddammit, Sophie hates seersucker, too! I swear I'll send it to a clothes bank tomorrow."

"Good. Of course I don't know you well, Captain Scott, but from what I've seen so far, I think you may be all right. Sophie could do a lot worse."

"Thank you," he said.

"Don't mention it!" She turned back to Spee. "All right," she said. "I'm ready now."

"Then take my hand."

She took it.

"And turn with me."

She turned, and for a curious moment seemed not to be anywhere, and then was in cool damp air.

They were standing outside a rather splendid Georgian house, its lower rooms ablaze with light.

"What on earth — wait, I know. Time and relative dimensions in space, yes?"

"Yes, if you like," Father Spee said, smiling.

"It feels like when they describe apparating — in the Harry Potter books."

"Ah, yes, the admirable Ms. Rowling. One would be wise not to underestimate her! Now — you see that house?"

"Yes."

"Someone you know lives there."

"Oh? Who?"

"Superintendent James Hanlon."

SIXTY-TWO

*R.A.F. Harlsden. The Control Capsule for Alfa 1.
About the same time.*

The second android, two kilometers distant in Alfa-1, had registered precisely when the will of its twin was challenged. In that awareness, it knew also the exact moment when that will was finally frustrated, the enabling codes could no longer be sent, and the launch sequence could not be completed. The operation had failed. At once, the android withdrew. Back through the passage, up to the ground level, back through the gate, to be joined by its twin.

Within minutes they had quit the compound. The creatures were now blind, guided by a single beacon—their point of origin. Programmed to destroy, they were returning to the one who dispatched them. Having failed in their errand of destruction, they would destroy their source. They no longer stuck to the winding road but smashed their way straight through the woodland, crashing through thicket and soaking brushwood and puddles, making in a direct line for Sherwood Road and the home of James Hanlon.

***

Capsule Alpha-2, some minutes later

David blinked and turned to his friend.

"Are you all right?" Lance said.

"Sure," David said. "You?"

"Sure."

"I think I must have dozed off for a minute—just standing there. Weird. I don't usually do that sort of thing." He went to his usual place, and sat down. "What's that smell, Lance? Did something die in here?"

"Maybe something's died in the air vents. Better tell maintenance, I guess."

"Yeah, maybe." David rubbed his ankle.

Then something caught his attention on the console. He got up, looked again at it, and tensed.

"For God's sake, Lance! Look! We're showing an aborted launch sequence. What the hell's happened?"

As he spoke, the phone rang. It was John, from Alfa-1. To judge by his voice, Lance figured he was just a couple of degrees this side of apoplexy.

SIXTY-THREE

London. The Academy for Philosophical Studies.
A few minutes later.

In his study at the academy, the chairman stood by the window and told himself to concentrate.

The television set, muted, offered an endless stream of banal images—late night talk shows, reruns, old movies. Those images would change at once when there was breaking news, and certainly they would change for the news he expected.

For now, he needed to concentrate.

And the truth was, his concentration was disturbed.

He could not know precisely what was happening to his androids when they were away from him. But the consultant had shown him how to adjust his thoughts so as to stay in a kind of contact with them for so long as they were active. Some minutes ago, however, his consciousness of them had become confused and troubled. All he could sense was their frustration. Yet he had done everything that the consultant had said was necessary. So what could have gone wrong?

Nonetheless, he was still able to sense them, and their frustration itself provided him with a strong link to them, perhaps stronger than ever. So he concentrated on that, willing them to greater strength, placing at their disposal all the depths of his own desire. He thought with longing of the moment of horror when the missiles would come in, the moment of terror: and then, of annihilation.

Purity of heart is to will one thing.

All might yet be ill.

Sixty-Four

Sherwood Road. A few minutes later.

"Here then is the next thing you are to do," Spee said, "Superintendent Hanlon — you must help him."

"*Me*? Help *him*?"

"Oh, yes. You are the person to do it, Cecilia Anna Maria. Especially you. Especially Hanlon. For you have something to forgive him."

"Not as much as Verity Jones."

"That is true. But Verity is a gentle, forgiving soul. She finds it quite easy to forgive. You, I think, do not."

"No I don't, especially when someone hurts my friends. But in any case it's not my place to forgive him for what he did to Verity. Only she can do that."

Spee smiled. "Very good! In another age and time you might have made a Jesuit. But Hanlon has injured you too, has he not? Or at least he tried to?"

She thought of her promotion.

"Yes," she said. "He did."

"Then you can forgive him for that."

"I could try. I can't pretend I'm not feeling pretty ticked off with him."

"Many people make this confusion. Cecilia Anna Maria, I'm not asking you to *feel* forgiving. That may come later. I'm asking you simply to forgive. It's as if someone owes you money but cannot pay, so you tear up his IOU. You may still *feel* ticked off with him, as you put it, but still, you've torn up the IOU, and so you've cancelled the debt—forgiven it. Could you do that with Hanlon?"

"I'm to say, 'Superintendent, you owe me and I'm ticked off with you, but I let you off. You don't have to pay.' Is that it?"

"Exactly!"

"All right. Consider it said. I'd like to beat him to a pulp and I bet I could. But I won't. All right?"

Spee smiled. "Yes. And incidentally, I bet you could, too. Now to your task. The thing you saw at the base, the android, the thing that was trying to launch the missiles? James Hanlon released it. In fact, he released the two of them."

"*Hanlon?* Hanlon organizing World War III? Father, I know you know a lot, but are you sure? He's an unpleasant little toad, but I find it hard to believe he's that smart."

"You are right. He isn't. Nor is he that wicked. Indeed he's not wholly bad. When he took his oath as a trainee police officer he meant it. He has some vision of an ordered world and he'd like to help create it. But like many people, to get the power and position he thinks will help him make his vision a reality, he's compromised. In particular, he's allowed himself to become enmeshed with the academy, and now the academy has duped him. He *didn't* know the androids were designed to start a nuclear war. In fact he didn't know *what* they were designed to do, and there he's culpable because he didn't ask. He thought he was being promised what he wanted and so he did as he was told. But now the androids and their plan of destruction have failed, and since they are programmed to destroy something, they're on their way back to destroy him, the one who released them. So Superintendent Hanlon needs your help."

"But how can I help?"

"You can stop them."

"Captain Scott and I between us could barely manage *one* of them just now, and even then we wouldn't have done it without Figaro. And now you think I can deal with two of them by myself?"

"I do not merely think it, I know it. This time it will actually be easy for you. You now have something in you that they will not be able to face. Trust me. I see it."

"All right. If you say so. I'll have a shot at it."

"You will have a shot at it and you will succeed. And when it is over I will come for you and take you home."

SIXTY-FIVE

The same. A few minutes later.

Cecilia went through the tall gates and along the drive toward the house, which as she approached appeared even larger and more impressive than she'd thought at first—"somewhat out of our price range" as Papa would have said. She mounted the steps to the porch and rang the bell.

Somewhere in the house something chimed.

A pause. Footsteps. The door opened.

Cecilia recognized at once the tall, well-dressed woman who answered it. Alison Hanlon was carrying a kitten, which she tried to put down. The kitten was in no mood to be put down and attached himself to her with a lifetime grip of his tiny claws. Finally she gave up and looked at Cecilia apologetically.

"Can I help you?"

"I'm so sorry to bother you late at night, Mrs. Hanlon," Cecilia said. "I'm sure you don't remember me, but we did meet once, at the police ball last year."

The woman smiled. "Why yes, now I look at you I do remember you rather clearly. You are Detective Inspector Cecilia Cavaliere. And you work for my husband, don't you?"

"I do, Mrs. Hanlon. Most people don't have such a good memory for faces."

"Most faces aren't quite so handsome as yours, nor do most people have such fine eyes."

"Oh, well, you're very kind."

"Don't mention it. I try only to give compliments when they're deserved. I gather, though, that my husband doesn't like you much, nor you him."

"Yes I'm afraid that's true, Mrs. Hanlon, and I'm sorry about it, but—"

"Oh please don't apologize my dear! I don't like him much myself. How can I help you? I'm afraid it'll have to be me. James seems to be rather unwell at the moment. I'm not really sure what's wrong with him."

"I know. I've come to help."

"Really? Well you'd better come in then."

Alison Hanlon, still encumbered with the kitten, led the way. Cecilia found herself in wide, lofty room that could, like the house, be described as splendid, although somewhat over-furnished. By the fireplace, hunched in a large armchair, James Hanlon sat staring into space.

He looked up as Cecilia entered. His face twisted with fury and he sprang to his feet.

"Cavaliere, how dare you come to my house! Alison, get that woman out of here!"

"Superintendent Hanlon," Cecilia said, "I need to tell you that I forgive you for trying to stop my promotion. I don't find it easy, but I do. I cancel your debt. And Verity Jones, I think she forgives you, too, because she's a forgiving soul. And now—"

"Damn you, woman, I don't need to be 'forgiven' by my junior officers and I'll thank you to—"

"But sir, you do need it and there really isn't time to argue about it. You see, those creatures you released earlier, well, they're coming back, and I'm afraid they're coming back for you. So—"

At that moment the kitten leapt out of Alison Hanlon's arms onto the carpet. Every hair on its body stood on end, its back arched, and it snarled, hissed, and spat furiously in the direction of the French windows — which were rattling.

"Look!" Cecilia pointed.

The catches shook. Then the double doors crashed inwards, splintering and shattering, leaving a gaping, dusty hole through which something entered. Some *things*.

Things that waddled toward them over shards of glass and broken wood, reeking malevolence and the odor of rotting flesh.

Alison Hanlon screamed.

The kitten stood its ground and screeched with rage.

Sixty-Six

The same. Seconds later.

James Hanlon groaned.

In one shattering instant the sight of the creatures he had released tore from him every illusion. He knew that he and Alison were to die and he saw with perfect clarity that the presence of the things that would kill them was his achievement.

How could he possibly have convinced himself that those vile creatures he had been persuaded to release could have had any good purpose? How could he have so stubbornly dismissed not just Cavaliere's doubt about the academy, but his own feelings about the way it treated him? Why had he ignored his own anger? His sense of humiliation? How could he not have been suspicious of the things they had asked him to do, such as the breaking of normal procedures with evidence on at least one occasion?

His dreams had led him to ignore all those questions and doubts.

And now all the perfumes of Arabia would not cleanse him.

Cecilia stepped to the center of the room, placing herself next to the kitten, between the androids and their intended victims.

The androids gazed directly into her eyes.

She gazed back.

In the capsule she'd been frightened, but now she could see more clearly. What poor, pathetic things they were. Misshapen. Deprived.

Somewhat to her surprise, she felt sorry for them.

The androids were confused. The one they were to destroy was there, to be sure, and seemed terrified. And there was another—equally fearful, equally ripe for destruction. Their programming had prepared them for all that.

But there was a third.

The creatures hesitated.

They sought to control the mind of this third as they had controlled other minds—and reeled at what they found there. Anger they had been programmed to handle. Or curiosity. Or fear. Even resistance such as one of them had encountered earlier in the capsule. All these they had been programmed to contain and, one way or another, to overcome or circumvent.

But they had not been programmed to deal with pity. Their data banks contained nothing whatever about pity—and for good reason: pity was a concept quite alien to their creator. So, encountering pity, his creatures were at a loss.

Of course the androids could not be redeemed, even by pity, for they had never really existed. Encountering pity they simply disintegrated: and, disintegrating, were freed from the endless dreariness of their semi-existence.

Left on the carpet were two unpleasant little heaps of evil-smelling dirt and what looked like a couple of computer chips—the secret, Cecilia surmised, of the creatures apparent ability to read and control the technology they encountered. But there was nothing that could not be cleared away with other rubbish when the room was cleaned.

The danger gone, the kitten recovered from its rage as quickly as it had been possessed by it, and rubbed itself round her ankles, purring raucously. She knelt for a moment to caress the tiny impassioned creature, gentle fingers scratching the arched furry back and the little round head.

She looked up at Alison Hanlon. "Is it a male or a female?"

"Male."

"What's his name?"

"Tiger."

"A good name!" She addressed the kitten. "Tiger, you were brave. I'm proud of you! I have to admit I'm a dog person myself, but a dear friend of mine has cats and I can certainly see that you're a fine cat. A *very* fine cat!"

There was a sound of chimes from the front door. She stood.

"I think that's my transport," she said, "so I have to go now. But I don't think there'll be any more trouble."

"You go, my dear," Alison Hanlon said. "I'll take care of him. Thank you for coming. And you really do have magnificent eyes. No wonder my husband is intimidated by you."

Left alone with her husband, who had sunk back into his chair, Alison gazed down at him.

"So," she said, "let's get this clear, James. Of course I've known for years that you're a chauvinistic pig, you married me for my money, and you can't keep your hands off any woman who's attractive. But now let's add what's come out this evening. You tried to cheat Cecilia Cavaliere out of her promotion, you've obviously done something nasty to that nice, bright little Verity Jones, and you were responsible for those two revolting creatures that came here tonight, did all this damage, and scared the hell out of me. Have I got that about right?"

But James Hanlon was for the moment a broken man. He could only stare at her.

"Well then, I think in the present circumstance we can reasonably assume silence means consent."

The kitten pawed at her ankle. She picked him up, whereupon he climbed onto her shoulder and promptly went to sleep.

"Now, here's what you're going to do..."

Sixty-Seven

The Hanlons' porch. A few minutes later.

Spee met Cecilia on the doorstep.

"I promised I would return you to your family if I could, and I can. So are you ready to apparate again?"

"I am. And is that the end of it?"

"No it is not. Then I shall go to Michael. Now there is something that *he* must do."

"Is it dangerous?"

"Of course. It's always dangerous to challenge evil. It is only more dangerous not to."

"Can't I do it?"

"No, it must be him. But you can pray for him, as he has been praying for you the whole evening."

"I'm not much good at praying. I'm better at doing things."

"Are you indeed? Well do this: think about Michael and wish him well and safe and commend him to God. Can you do that?"

"Yes, I think so."

"Do that and you will be praying. And remember, in this as in all things, when we try to be obedient, *et Spiritus adiuvat infirmitatem nostram* — the Spirit also helpeth our infirmity. Now come, take my hand, and turn as you did before."

"Wait!" she said, "Please?"

He looked at her.

"Look," she said, "what you said—I do wish him well and safe and I do commend him to God. But I can do that anywhere, can't I?"

"Of course you can."

"So why can't I do it *there*, with him? I hear you say he's the one who's got to do this, whatever it is, and I'm not arguing about that, but why can't I just at least be with him? So he knows? Like I knew he was praying for me."

"You want to stand with him his peril? To *share* his danger?"

"Yes," she said. "I do. I want to do that. I want to be with him."

He looked at her hard and shook his head. But he was smiling, and there seemed to be tears in his eyes.

"Cecilia Anna Maria, you have a great heart," he said. "You have won me. Come."

SIXTY-EIGHT

London. The Lady Chapel of St. Andrew's, Holborn Circus.
A minute later.

Michael Aarons realized that he was no longer alone in the Lady Chapel.

He rose to his feet and turned to see a man in a black cloak — dark hair touched with gray, dark bearded, a little past his youth. He knew who it was. He'd seen his picture earlier that evening.

"You are Father Friedrich Spee von Langenfeld of the Society of Jesus."

Spee inclined his head in acknowledgment.

"And you are Father Michael Aarons," he said. "You don't seem surprised to see me."

"I know that departed saints are sometimes sent to the faithful in times of crisis. Perhaps this is such a time."

Spee nodded and gave Michael a faint smile.

"Yes, though I must point out that I am a departed saint only in that I am of the baptized. Not, I think, in any more exalted sense."

"Perhaps, Father, that isn't for you to decide."

Spee smiled again, broadly this time.

"Perhaps not. You are quite right. And now Father, here is your friend, Cecilia Anna Maria."

Cecilia stepped out of the shadow.

"Hello, Michael."

His heart leapt with pleasure.

"Cecilia! You're all right!"

"Yes!"

"But how on earth—?"

She grinned at him and took his hands.

"Don't even go there! It's something to do with relative dimensions in time and space. Isn't that right, Father?"

Spee smiled and nodded. "Something to do with that, yes."

"Papa says somebody's explained it. Except," she added after a moment's further consideration, "they don't seem to know how to do it—not without blowing up a star."

"Good heavens," Michael said.

"But the thing is, I'm here. All right?"

"Absolutely!"

"Cecilia Anna Maria has helped to prevent a great evil," Spee said. "But now there remains the one who tried to set this evil in motion. The guiding mind, here in this city. A man who has given himself to darkness. It is not the will of our Beloved that he should perish. It is not the will of our Beloved that any should perish. And this is your task. Cecilia Anna Maria wishes to come with you, but the task is yours."

Michael nodded.

"Tell me what to do," he said.

"He has learned to harness certain powers of earth, powers to which he has no right and which are destructive even to him, though he is too far gone in his madness to mind that. But he will seek to use them against you. You must both be armed against those. And, if you will, we shall all pray together. But even before that there is something I must tell you—for you, Michael Aarons, are much more closely connected to this man than you know. And that is the special reason why this task is yours."

SIXTY-NINE

The Academy for Philosophical Studies. A little later.

For Michael Aarons the experience that night was in some respects vivid, in others like a dream: in some ways dramatic (at least for him), and in others quite prosaic. They prayed together with Father Spee in the Lady Chapel at Saint Andrew's, and then Spee told him and Cecilia truths about the chairman of the academy that stunned and surprised them. All that was rather dramatic. But then there was a walk under the streetlights from Saint Andrew's to Holborn Circus Underground Station—a walk such as Michael might have taken on any day or night of the week. He bought tickets and the three of them caught a late-night tube—the last one running, he rather thought—to Lancaster Gate. Perhaps, after all Cecilia's talk of time and relative dimensions, he had expected to travel in some more dramatic fashion, but it was not to be.

"We shall be in time," Father Spee said. "The urgent task is done, and that fellow at the academy will go on all night in pursuit of his foolish dream." Then he smiled. "Anyway, I like trains. There weren't any, in my day."

Another short walk and they were standing outside the Academy for Philosophical Studies. The air was cool, but not unpleasantly so.

Cecilia was staring across the road. Michael followed her gaze. She was looking at a parked Mercedes that gleamed metallically under the streetlight.

"What is it?" he said.

She frowned slightly, then shook her head.

"It doesn't matter," she said. "We know why we're here."

"That's true," Spee said, also following her gaze, "but still, Cecilia Anna Maria, you are quite right. You *have* seen that car before—in Exeter, just for moment, the day you quarreled with Superintendent Hanlon." He shook his head. "You really *are* very good! I should not like to be a criminal pursued by you!"

He turned to face them both. "But now," he said, "to the task! You must be armed. I want you both to look up. Look at the heavens. Look at the stars."

Surprised at the abrupt change of subject, Michael nonetheless did as Spee instructed. The clouds that covered the sky earlier in the evening had rolled back. Between them he could just discern one or two of the brightest stars, though even they were rendered faint by light pollution from the city.

"You see them better in the country," Cecilia said.

"Yes," Spee said. "You do. But do you hear them?"

"Hear them?" she said.

"Do you mind if I touch your heads?"

"No, Father."

"Then listen."

Spee took their right hands and gently brought them together, then reached up and placed his left hand on Cecilia's head, his right on Michael's. Michael felt the gentle, warm pressure through his hair.

And then he heard—or more than heard, for every one of his senses was ravished with sweetness and glory. It was music beyond music, the melody of love beyond love. Solemn and merry, awful and gentle, it poured into him, and his whole being tingled with delight. It seemed to him that he was no longer looking upwards or outwards at the stars, at space, the infinite beyond, but rather that he was looking *into* these things, into a vast glory of which the earth, the solar system, the galaxy, the entire universe as he knew it were merely outposts, drops in an ocean, a beginning. And for the first time in his life he felt that he understood — really understood — what the psalmist had meant when he said, *ha-shamaim mesapherim kevod-el* — the heavens declare God's glory.

Spee removed his hand, and after a few seconds Michael could no longer hear the music, though the knowledge of it and the joy of it remained, and even the silence was rich with its influence.

He turned to Cecilia. There were tears on her cheeks, but her eyes were shining. She gave a deep sigh and smiled at him and squeezed his hand, at all of which he thought his heart would break with pleasure. He felt more alive than he could have imagined possible. He felt strong — no, that was a massive understatement — he felt as if he could, quite literally, have done anything.

Spee smiled. "There!" he said. "You have heard the music."

"Is that what they call the music of the spheres?" Michael said.

"*Musica universalis.* Yes." He turned to Cecilia. "It's what *you* heard in the cathedral."

Cecilia smiled and nodded, but she said nothing.

"The fact is," Spee said, "the universe isn't just empty space and rarified gasses. It isn't just subatomic particles. All that's only what it is made of. The universe is a *dance*. Some of your physicists have begun to see that. It's an enchanted and everlasting dance. And we were created to be part of it. See how it's filled you both with joy, and you've only had the tiniest glimpse of it!

"Now go with God. I don't think anyone who's just heard what you've heard will easily be overthrown by the tricks of the enemy."

Michael mounted the porch and as he touched the doors they opened. He entered the academy, Cecilia following.

SEVENTY

Inside the academy.

The entrance hall was well lit. Two men in the gray uniforms of a securities firm were sitting playing cards at a desk. As Michael and Cecilia walked in they both looked up.

"Excuse me, sir, but—"

"You should both leave," Michael said quietly. "It would be best to do it now."

Without a word the two got to their feet and left, filing past Michael and Cecilia without a backward glance.

Michael watched them.

"Well," he said, "that was easy."

Cecilia gave him a little smile.

"I love it when you're bossy," she said.

Together they mounted dimly lit, heavily carpeted stairs, flight after flight, landing by landing to the fifth floor, and so came to a heavy mahogany door. It bore a brass plate on which was the one word, "Chairman."

Michael raised his hand and touched it.

Like the front doors, it opened at once.

The chairman, still watching the television and the window, was suddenly conscious of a presence—an unwelcome presence.

He turned.

The door to his office was open. How could that be?

In the doorway stood a slim, slightly built figure. In flickering light the tall man could see his face: lean, clean shaven, and marked with lines of pain. He appeared to be a priest or minister of some kind. Slightly behind him was a woman with long, dark hair.

This was intolerable.

He walked to his desk and pressed a button. "Security to my office," he said. "At once."

"There is no security," the priest said. "I have relieved them of duty."

Again the chairman pressed the button. "Security! Chairman's office! Now!"

"You can rant and shout all you like," the priest said. "They aren't coming. I told you. I've relieved them of duty."

The chairman felt rage rising within him, boiling and seething.

He gave himself to it, and as he did so raised his hand and pointed. For a moment nothing happened. Then from his fingers leapt fire that flickered for several seconds around his hand, then flared and enveloped the strangers. It was a power that he had achieved over decades, and he rarely dared to use it: his focused fury creating an excess of energy that produced combustion.

But when the fire died the intruders were still there. They appeared to be unscathed.

Again the chairman concentrated upon his rage, again the fingers pointed, again the fire leapt, and again the strangers were enveloped. This time he let the fire burn long minute upon long minute. The carpet around them began to smolder.

But when at last, his body screaming in protest, he could sustain the flames no longer, the intruders were still there, and unscathed.

"That's impressive," the priest said. "You've learned a trick with muscle mitochondria and calcium sparks. But it's quite useless against us—surely you can see that? And since it's unnatural, it's deadly to you. If you do it many more times, it will kill you."

The chairman frowned. What the priest said was true. And while he did not care about his own destruction, he was loath to invoke it before his project was complete.

So despite himself he asked, "Why have you come? Who are you?"

"I've come because it is not the will of our Beloved that anyone should perish. And I've been sent to warn you."

"To warn *me*?" The chairman felt his confidence returning. Evidently, though the pair before him knew some tricks, they did not know what mattered. "Then those who sent you are fools and so are you. Do you know what I have done? Do you have any idea? They have cities to warn. Nations. Why should they warn *me*?"

"They know what you've done—better than you, actually. And so do I. Feel your creatures."

Michael watched as the chairman, for the first time, looked shaken.

"It is true that I lost contact with them some time ago," he said. "But it is of no importance. They have been programmed. They cannot be stopped."

"They just were. A young American airman and this woman—Cecilia, my friend—they did it."

"That is nonsense. A joke. I assure you no weapon at present existing on this planet can stop the androids."

"Yes, it is a bit of a joke, isn't it? All your money and resources and diabolic machinations—oh, sorry, of course, you don't believe in God or devil, do you?—well anyway, all your cleverness smashed up by two brave people with no resources at all but their courage and their honor."

"Thank you," Cecilia whispered in his ear. "But don't forget Figaro!"

"Oh, yes, and a dog. Cecilia reminds me quite properly that at a crucial moment in last night's operation against your androids, vital assistance was provided by a hairy black dog called Figaro. Does that make you feel better? You're quite right—it's a joke. And of course that's exactly why you can't see it. You've no sense of humor. You never had. You've always taken yourself so *seriously*. Still, what I'm here for isn't a joke. As I said, I've come to warn you. You've only minutes left. This place is doomed and at the moment so are you. But *you* can still be saved. No one wants your destruction. All you have to do is repent."

"*Repent?*"

"Yes. You can choose remorse for all the evil you've done. I suggest you start with something easy. Remember your little sister Elisabeth? Remember how she loved you and looked up to you? Remember she wanted you to come to her birthday party? And you quite wanted to go, because there were going to be strawberry ices, and you liked strawberry ices. But then you found out that when you said you wouldn't go, it made her cry, and you liked that even better. Can you imagine that? A little boy so silly so petty and pathetic he'd rather make his sister cry than eat strawberry ices? Yet that was you, and you've gone on like it ever since, never growing up properly, just getting nastier and nastier. But Elisabeth still wants you to come to her party. She *has* grown up, and she constantly prays for you in the divine Presence."

"How *dare* you speak to me of such a person!"

"I dare very easily."

"You know nothing of me."

"Oh, you're wrong there. I know quite a lot about you. To tell the truth, I know a good deal more about you than I want to know, but it can't be helped. To start with, I know how old you are. And I know your name, S. S. Oberleutnant Heinrich Weis."

For a moment the chairman was silent.

"You are a Jew," he said at last. "I knew it. Why do you dress like a Christian priest?"

"Certainly I'm a Jew. I'm a Jew like Saint Paul—I've found the Messiah. So I'm also a Christian priest. But that's my story, and we're not here to talk about my story except as it's linked to yours. My name is Michael Aarons, and you owe my family blood, Heinrich Weis—you owe them for Bergen-Belsen, where you and your kind let them die of typhoid and starvation. Starvation was your cure for diarrhea, wasn't it? 'If they don't eat, they won't shit,' you said, and thought yourselves no end clever and witty. In a way Belsen was worse than Auschwitz, for at least the gas chambers were quick. That was an achievement, wasn't it? You managed to create something worse than Auschwitz! How about that! And inside it, along with thousands of others, almost every member of my family died except my grandfather, who was only nine years' old, and an aunt, who was about fourteen. They managed somehow to survive until the British came and rescued them. But they had those blue identification numbers on their arms for the rest of their lives."

Now the chairman's mouth twisted.

"Then undoubtedly we should have had them killed while we had the chance."

"Perhaps you should. So far as I know neither of them ever claimed it as any particular merit in them that they'd survived. But that's their story and as I just said, what matters now is *your* story. I come in the name of my family and of many others—whose blood is upon you and who now rejoice in the Presence of Ha-Shem. And they authorize me to offer you their forgiveness. They cancel your debt to them. They too, with your sister Elisabeth, remember you before the Throne. Oh, and there's Johnny—John Stewart Cox, who bumped into you in the academy and said rude things about the lectures. We've just learned you had a man paid to kill him. You ended a beautiful young life for something so trivial that he'd forgotten about it. Why did you do that, Heinrich?"

The chairman snorted. "He was unimportant!"

Michael sighed. "No one is unimportant. Why did you do it?"

"I did it because I could, and because he was insolent. He publicly offended me. And I was clever. I even had the killer take no weapon but use what he found there, so the police were fooled into looking for a mere burglar who had murdered by accident."

"Oh, *very* adroit," came softly from just behind Michael's left ear. "I expect he'll want a bloody medal for that."

Michael could not entirely contain a half smile.

"Well, Heinrich," he said, "I have to tell you that John Stewart Cox, *unimportant* John Stewart Cox, forgives you, too. He's another who's cancelled your debt to him. And he prays for you. Monotonous, isn't it? You see, Heinrich, it's mercy all, immense and free, and there's no getting away from it, however hard you try."

"Mercy and forgiveness are for the defeated," the tall man said. "These things are the morality of the weak, of slaves."

Michael shook his head. "We've no time for this," he said. "Heinrich Weis, you will look into my eyes."

It seemed to the chairman that the priest, though smaller in stature than himself, was suddenly greater than he. And in that moment—despite himself, despite his own will—the chairman saw. He saw blood, streaming in the firmament, streaming in compassion and pardon from a broken figure on a cross outside Jerusalem. He saw every single one of the lives that he had destroyed now drawn into the arms of a mercy that gave them glory. He saw an infinite price paid for all—and even for him. He sensed the Creator he denied, the Creator who yearned for his joy. He sensed divine pity and agony over creation. He seemed to hear a voice: *In all their afflictions, God was afflicted.*

He began to tremble.

SEVENTY-ONE

The Infernal City.

In his suite of offices on the senior executive floor of Central Administration, the consultant considered the stream of information coming in to him via the array of screens above his desk.

And frowned.

It was not that he was particularly troubled by the failure of the androids and the collapse of the chairman's plans to start a nuclear war. To be sure, he had no objection to such a war — indeed, he'd looked forward to it. Wars of any kind generally led to a good deal of cruelty and suffering, and were therefore amusing. But that was all. Though entertaining in their short-term effects, they had little relevance to the Infernal City's over-all purpose — to seduce humanity from the One — and in some circumstances could even frustrate it. A man who'd been self-ish and cowardly all his life would suddenly go and get himself killed trying to help a wounded comrade under fire. A woman who'd never seemed interested in anything but her own com-fort would rush into a bombed and burning house and perish trying to rescue a baby — or even the cat! And in such cases the One had an infuriating habit of claiming them, asserting that in dying for another they'd followed, knowingly or not, the foot-steps of His Son! Sentimental claptrap!

No, what disturbed the consultant was not failure to start a war, but concern that he might lose the chairman himself. The wretched man had been granted a vision, a clear vision, at the hands of those who were professed servants of the One. And he had evidently seen it for what it was. He had understood it. How then would he react? Decades of work were in jeopardy. There was only one thing to be done. Serious threat called for serious response.

He must go and deal with the situation himself.

Reluctantly, the consultant rose to his feet, folded his wings, shimmered darkly for six-and-a-half seconds, and vanished.

Michael was suddenly aware that there was someone standing beside the chairman: a figure in shadow whom he could not see clearly. But the chairman saw him, and evidently knew him.

"Consultant?" he said. "How did you get here?"

"That does not matter," the figure said. "What matters is that *you* are losing control."

"Who *is* that?" Cecilia whispered to Michael.

"I don't know."

"I don't like him."

"Nor do I."

"This one talks prettily," the figure said, pointing to Michael. "He weaves spells and pleasing myths. Almost, one might believe him. But remember what we have always said. They are illusions. They mean nothing. There is no God, and there is no devil. There is only —"

"I think you've said enough."

Michael and Cecilia both swung round.

In the open doorway stood a woman.

SEVENTY-TWO

The academy, a moment later.

As the woman entered, Michael found himself gasping with delight at her mere presence. She radiated grace and joy. But she also radiated power. Out of the corner of his eye he saw that the one Weis called consultant had reeled back against the wall, cowering and covering his eyes.

So who was she? Surely Our Lady herself—?

"No," Cecilia whispered, evidently reading his thought but with sharper insight. "It's Heinrich Weis's sister."

It was.

"Elisabeth?" Heinrich said. "*You*?"

She laughed, her laughter an enchantment that pierced the heart. "Of course it's me. Did you think I'd forget you?"

Michael had the sense that she was speaking German, a language in which he was not fluent: yet he understood her perfectly.

"And now, dearest Heinrich," she said, "for Goodness's sake, *do* stop it!"

"What do you mean? Stop what?"

Heinrich still spoke his clipped, somewhat pedantic English, though his sister clearly had no difficulty following him.

"I mean stop all this nonsense and listen."

"Why?"

"Because I can teach you what you need to know. I can to teach you how to die. It's quite simple, really."

"I hardly need you to teach me that. I have been arranging it myself for some time."

"Heinrich, I don't mean self-murder—which, incidentally, you've no more right to do than you had to murder all those other people. I mean self-surrender. I mean dying into life."

"That is all nonsense. Mystical riddles. Death is death and life is life. One cannot die into life."

She laughed again. "Then what do you make of *me*, Heinrich? I died in the bombs at Dresden. You know I did."

"You are a figment of my imagination. A phantom."

"Oh, Heinrich!" She walked up to him, laid her hand upon his cheek, and gazed down into his face, for tall as he was, she was taller. And to Michael, seeing the two of them together, it appeared that it was Heinrich, not she, who was the phantom. The woman's hand, her face, her whole being radiated life, vigor, a transfigured corporeality so rich it made Heinrich seem to be only half there, his outline blurred. Insofar as he was solid at all, it was the solidarity of a skeleton. He had no face. The long, beautiful fingers were caressing bone.

"Heinrich," Elisabeth said softly, "just try for a moment to pay attention to something outside of yourself, will you?" She stroked his cheek. "Now, how do I feel to you? Do I *feel* like a phantom?"

"Of course not. That is part of the dream. But you do not exist. You do not exist because you cannot exist. You died. And that is why you talk in riddles—*dying into life*! Mystical claptrap."

"Oh, Heinrich, *wake up!*" Without warning the glorious creature whipped back her hand and struck him, hard and fast across the bony cheek.

"Aagghh!" He reeled back. "You bloody little bitch!" For a moment his form became distinct, and he spoke German.

It seemed the blow had cost his sister some effort. Her face showed pain. But it disappeared as quickly as it came, and her voice when she spoke was again music, and now with a hint of mirth, as if she were inviting him to share the joke.

"There, Heinrich! Are you *still* sure I don't exist?"

"*Of course you do not!*" There was no mirth in Heinrich. He screamed at her, though in comparison with the melody of her speech his scream was pale and bloodless. And again he was back to English. "It is all nonsense and I will not have it. I am simply having a particularly vivid dream."

Again his outline had become blurred, skeletal.

She gazed at him and shook her head. "What a shame!" she said. "They tell me a sudden shock works sometimes."

"You foolish girl, stop staring at me! When you were a child you were always staring at me with your big, stupid eyes!"

"I stared at you because you were my big brother and I thought you were wonderful. Now I'm staring at you because you're rather hard for me to see. It's not just the situation, you know. I mean — look at your friends!" To Michael's surprise she turned to bestow a ravishing smile on him and Cecilia. "*You're* both quite clear to me. I can see you quite well. In fact, I think you must have been listening to the music. But *you*," she turned back to her brother, "Heinrich, I can hardly see you at all."

"Go away," he said. "You are an illusion. I have always insisted on reality."

"No, Heinrich, you haven't." She sighed. "You've just taken hold of one little bit of reality that you didn't at all understand and you've fed it and worshipped it until it swelled to madness and gave you an excuse to be cruel, which for some reason you seem to enjoy. Yes, what you're always saying — monotonously saying, I'm afraid: you really have become a most frightful bore — anyway, what you say is true. All things die. But can't you see? The universe isn't only full of death, it also *throbs* with resurrection. Even if you couldn't see it before, you can see it now. You can see it if you *let* yourself see it. Just *look* at me, Heinrich."

"Do you mock me with your beauty?"

This time, Michael noticed, he did not tell her she was an illusion.

"No, Heinrich dearest, I want you to *share* it. All you've got to do is admit you've done some wicked things and say you're sorry. Then you can begin to grow and be happy. There'll be some growing pains, but I'll help you with those and I promise you won't mind them a bit."

"So what you are saying is, you will allow me to be happy just so long as I follow your rules?"

"Heinrich, they're not *my* rules! But an orchestra can't play if it's not in tune. You can't dance if you won't move to the music. And waiting for you are joys for evermore—whatever your silly consultant says!"

It was the first time she'd acknowledged the consultant's presence since her own mere presence had silenced him when she entered. He'd been motionless since then, cowering in the shadows. Now she looked at him directly, and again he shrank before her, as if he feared she might strike him as she had struck her brother. But she only gazed at him thoughtfully, and rather sadly, as it seemed to Michael. At last she sighed and turned back to her brother.

"This is so sad. Such glory wasted. I can't think why you listen to him. He's a liar. He's been lying to you from the beginning. Oh Heinrich, dear, dear Heinrich, do you *really* not believe me?"

SEVENTY-THREE

The same, a minute later.

The consultant gasped, appalled. He could not, dare not, challenge her. She was utterly beyond his grasp, radiating such power that he, former archangel and present lord of the infernal city though he was, could scarcely stand in her presence. When she looked at him directly just now he'd thought for a moment that he would sink down before her — and indeed he *would* have done so, had she not taken pity on him (it galled him to admit it, but he'd seen the pity in her eyes) and looked away just in time for him to hold onto his dignity. And the fact was, Heinrich Weis clearly *did* believe her. Half a century of work was crumbling.

He must act.

"So," he whispered into Weis's ear, averting his eyes lest they meet those of that terrible sister, "it seems we have been wrong. There *is* a God. We grant it. We believe, and tremble. But then we must pose a question — what use has he been? He wasn't much use to all those people you killed in Bergen-Belsen, was he? And most of them claimed to believe in him! Not much use to Johnny Cox, either! Not much use to anyone, when it comes down to it. He couldn't save his own Son! So why kowtow to him now? Because he's sent a Jew priest and your prissy little dead sister to plead with you? Is that the best he can do? Who needs such a God?" The consultant became more insinuating. "What's the matter with you, man? Assert your independence! Claim your power! *Make the silly little bitch cry, just like you've always done!* You'll never have such an opportunity again."

It was a desperate throw.

But it was all he could think of.

And it was working.

He watched, fascinated, as the old fool took the bait.

As it dawned on Heinrich Weis that even now he could vomit on the grace and beauty before him.

As he relished the thought of once more making his sister cry.

As he saw how he could slap her down, despite her new-found airs and graces!

And those others — the Jew priest and the woman — they too would be humiliated.

All right — so there was a God. What of it? He, Heinrich Weis, possessed power to thwart that God, to frustrate the divine purpose.

And he would use it.

The consultant watched it all and smiled.

Am I good at this, or am I good at it?

In the instant that Weis made his choice, the priest and the woman were gone from him.

So was his sister.

Save for the consultant, he was alone.

A second later the fire was around him.

"It has come!" he shouted. "I have humiliated you all! I have defied destiny! I have triumphed over God!"

"So you have," the consultant said soothingly, "and now we can go home. Nothing need ever disturb you again."

Seventy-Four

The academy, a few minutes later.

Where there is offering in hell the price must be paid or the one who offers must forfeit. This is one of Lucifer's own rules, and he insists on it. Heinrich Weis, who acknowledged neither creator nor devil, had yet in some perverse way recognized the law of hell, and the consultant, who of course knew that law perfectly well, had made sure that he act in accord with it. So Weis had been persuaded to use Hanlon as his tool to launch the androids precisely as a shield for Weis himself. If anything went wrong it would be Hanlon, not Weis, who had set them on their way, and so Hanlon who would pay the forfeit. What Weis had not bargained for — what not even the consultant had bargained for — was that the androids themselves might be destroyed when as yet no life had been given. But that was exactly what had happened. So now the power behind the androids turned, as it was bound to, on Weis himself as the one who had invoked it.

The weather in London during May of 2009 was generally calm and rather warmer than usual. For the first time since 1996, no thunderstorms were observed and the winds were never more than moderate, becoming steadily warmer as the month moved on. Anyone who cares to check the records of London weather for the year 2009 can see all this. There was, however, one exception. A small part of the area known as Bayswater experienced a freak electrical storm on the night of the 25th May. So extraordinary and unexpected was this storm, so brief its duration and so limited its effects, that not surprisingly some records simply omit it as being of no relevance to, and having had no effect on, the overall picture. For what the statistic is worth, its duration was 11.185272 seconds and its effect, for all practical purposes, was limited to a single bolt of lightning that crashed with appalling ferocity on just one of a row of rather gracious Victorian houses in an avenue off the Bayswater Road—the home, as it happened, of the Academy for Philosophical Studies.

Within seconds the entire edifice was wrapped in fire.

Once before, an upper chamber of that house had been cleansed by fire from heaven, but that to this was as a summer breeze to a tornado.

There was much about the blaze that appeared to defy rational explanation. The London Fire Brigade, the largest and surely one of the most efficient and best-equipped organizations of its kind in the world, was there within minutes. Six appliances (as the London firefighting vehicles are known) poured thousands of gallons of water onto the conflagration, and experienced firefighters made every possible effort. But virtually nothing was saved—certainly not the building, which was razed to the ground.

The great consolation was that despite the intensity of the fire, perhaps in part through the skilled work of the fire service, the two terrace houses adjoining the academy were scarcely damaged at all, their paintwork barely scorched. Some who recalled the London blitz from their childhood said they remembered the occasional similarly freakish effect of a German bomb. It was as if just one piece, a house-sized slice, had been carved out of the row with a giant knife.

Also remarkable was the fact that practically everyone in the place got out. Two security men had left the building minutes before the storm, although neither of them could quite remember why. One seemed to think maybe he'd had a mad desire for a cigarette, which was not permitted in the building. Whatever the reason, they were both standing outside, smoking, when the lightning struck.

There was one casualty—someone who, so the experts reckoned, must at the moment of the lightning strike have been in the chairman's office. Charred fragments of a man's corpse were found as inspectors sifted through debris the following day.

The fragments could not be identified.

SEVENTY-FIVE

R.A.F. Harlsden. Tuesday, May 26th. Morning.

Though no one on the base—other than Lance Scott—had any recollection of the androids' incursion, everyone knew that something had gone wrong. Within minutes of the Alpha-1 and Alpha-2 crews becoming aware of the aborted launch sequence, Communications Command and Control lines between R.A.F. Harlsden, the R.A.F. Headquarters in London, and the United States' Central Command Post in Little Rock, Arkansas, were buzzing. What, exactly, had happened? Who or what was behind it? Al Qaeda? Homegrown lunatics? The military's own error or negligence?

The most rigorous inquiry could find evidence of none of these things. There was no sign of any hostile incursion and no evidence of any failure on the part of security. For whatever reason, upon investigation it seemed that procedures at Harlsden had if anything been pursued *more* vigorously than usual. Yet the fact remained: something had malfunctioned. Failing a conspiracy involving virtually every person on the base—a scenario so improbable and hard to imagine that the officers in charge of the investigation decided it was simply out of the question—then the failure had to be with the system, and what *that* meant was a colossal headache for the technicians.

It was a headache they would be allowed to nurse for several months until eventually someone in authority would decide that since no munitions had been expended, no fuel had been used, no personnel had acted, and there had been no surge in electrical power—in other words, since from a military point of view nothing had happened—it was time to stop. The investigation would close and the dossier describing it would be filed.

On the first day of the investigation, Lance and David like everyone else on the base were obliged to play their part in the inquiry, and it was only toward evening that they were able to go off duty. Lance, as usual, drove them in the MG. The day had not been easy for him. He'd decided to say nothing of his experiences because he was sure that Father Spee was right— no one would believe him if he did. But it is never easy to know more than you are supposed to know, and especially when the issue is under inquiry. At no point, so far as he recalled, did he actually tell a direct lie, but he certainly said less than he could have said and refrained from explaining things he could have explained. Being by habit and preference a person who likes to have things out in the open, he found the restraint involved in all this quite exhausting.

But it was now a pretty evening, and the crisis being over (at least so far as he and David were concerned), his mood lightened. He looked forward to some free time. And above all he was looking forward to phoning Sophie, to refreshing himself in the sweetness of her voice.

And not just to phoning her.

The priest who had come to him in the capsule had been right. It was time to act.

The door we never opened

Into the rose garden.

He would *not* spend the rest of his life regretting that he had never tried to open the door.

All right, it might not work.

But, by God, at least he'd give it a shot.

They arrived at the pleasant Victorian house in Wonford Road where David had his lodgings, and Lance brought the car to a stop. As his friend prepared to get out, he could contain himself no longer.

"You know," he said, "I've been thinking. About Sophie."

"I reckon you're going to ask her to marry you," David said.

"That's exactly what I was going to say! How on earth did you know that?"

"I'm not sure." David grinned. "Somehow I just did. Wasn't someone saying to you just recently that you ought to marry her, if she'd have you? Yesterday, was it?" He paused for a moment, then shook his head. "Well, maybe I dreamed it. Anyway, I think perhaps you've been saying it yourself for quite a while, only just not aloud."

Lance stared at his friend for a moment.

"Well then, since you guessed my first bit, I suppose you'll guess the rest. I think we should get some good counseling together first."

"Good idea. It won't be easy for either of you, if you're going to make it work."

"That's what I thought." Lance smiled. "You read me like a book."

"No, not especially. But I do feel like I've had this conversation with you before, or heard you have it with someone." Lance looked at him, fascinated, but said nothing.

David got out of the car, tote bag in hand. Then he turned and looked down at his friend.

"Well," he said, "good night—and good luck to both of you! You're both completely crazy, so I expect between the pair of you you'll make it work. Stranger things have happened!"

SEVENTY-SIX

St. Andrew's Vicarage. The same morning.

Michael was in his study. It was daylight. The German eight-day clock on the wall stood at five to ten.

Puzzled, he looked round and at once saw Father Spee, who was standing by the big bay window, gazing down with evident pleasure and fascination at Holborn Circus, where the mid-morning London traffic rush was in full swing.

"What happened?" Michael said. "The last thing I remember was being with Cecilia and talking to that fellow in the academy and then his beautiful sister talking to him. But that was the middle of the night. Did I pass out or something? Did I screw it up?"

Spee turned from the window, smiled, and shook his head. "No, you did not screw it up. You all did everything you could have done, and the silly fellow refused. He'd still rather make his sister cry than eat ice cream. Of course he doesn't have that power over her any more. She is in Love and will not be out of it, so he can't actually hurt her. But for the rest he has what he has chosen. Our Beloved will woo but will never compel."

Michael nodded. In another context he had said much the same himself to Cecilia.

"To tell you the truth," he said, "I can hardly imagine how he did it, how he could possibly refuse her. I mean, I heard her call him—so sweetly, so strongly. It seems to me the strength of will needed to insist on damnation must be twenty times what's needed for blessedness."

"Does that surprise you? We were created for blessedness, for union with the Beloved. So every fiber of our being, every cell, every molecule, cries out against our refusing it."

"And yet he refused. And listened to that other fellow—the consultant."

"And yet he refused. And listened to that other fellow."

"So there's no hope for him?"

Spee shook his head. "I don't know. Who could have imagined our Beloved would take flesh and die for us, before it happened? Heinrich's sister Elisabeth—she is so far advanced in understanding and glory she had to travel further than you could conceive to be with him and plead with him: yet our Beloved bid her come and she came willingly. So who knows what else might be done? But for the moment Heinrich Weis has what he has chosen."

Again Michael nodded.

Then he said, "Why did you need us? Me? Cecilia?"

Spee gazed at him for a moment.

"Because," he said finally, "if evil in this world is to be truly confronted, then it must be by faithfulness and love from this world, not by intervention from outside it. That's one reason our Beloved took flesh. Love created the order of the universe and that order is sacred to Love. It's not to be broken or overwhelmed, even for Love's sake."

"But surely you just *did* intervene? And more than once?"

"We warned. God has always warned—through prophets, dreams, messengers—and always will."

"But Father, you did a lot more than just warn us."

Spee smiled and nodded.

"Forgive me," he said. "You are quite right. We *did* do more than warn you. That was because the enemies of life had already twisted and bent the universe's order for their own purposes.

And by that they'd gained powers to which they had no right. The creatures Lancelot and Cecilia Anna Maria faced were one result of that distortion. The dark fire that foolish man produced was another. And then of course that other — the dark angel he called 'consultant' — he had no right to be there at all."

He paused. Michael waited.

"And so," Spee continued, "simply to give ordinary human good will some possibility of challenging those powers, Love acted."

"So… what, exactly? We experienced miracles?"

"Yes. In the church militant such events as you have seen are properly called miracles."

"So then, to help us, our side also twisted the order of the universe?"

"No! Never that! Ask Cecilia Anna Maria, and she'll tell you — *even the Queen's under the law, for it's the law that makes her Queen.* So our Beloved is under the law — not in the same way, of course, for our Beloved created the law — but created not merely by bare fiat, as if might were right, but *secundum consilium voluntatis suae*, by the *counsel* of his will: created it because it's a law of love and joy."

"But — miracle?"

"Even with miracle, still our Beloved works *through* and *with* the created order — in ways, to be sure, that may transcend it but never in ways that violate or distort it. Our Beloved created us by a supernatural act and by another supernatural act extends our powers. But it's all in harmony.

"As for what happened last night? As well as warning you, we enabled you to be where you needed to be but couldn't have been, or at least not in time if you were to act. And we were allowed to give you a brief vision of reality that would strengthen you against the false powers of Heinrich Weis. But we did nothing more. It was *human* courage that defeated the creatures at the base. It was *human* compassion that overwhelmed them at Superintendent Hanlon's house. And it was *human* calls to repentance that gave Heinrich his chance of life—the chance he refused. Even his sister Elisabeth, for all the wonder of her growing life in Christ, for all the power of grace that enabled her to be with him, yet once there, made her plea simply as his sister, speaking out of human, sisterly love. Yes, our Beloved acted in all these things, but in and through all of you, and your faith."

"Faith, yes. And that's another thing," Michael said. "You being around—honestly, it's made it much easier than usual to believe."

"*While* I'm around, yes!" Spee smiled. "But once I'm gone—you'd find it remarkably easy to explain me away, if you want to. Remember, the knowledge you get from religious experience is real knowledge, but to understand it and sustain it you have to accept it, to commit yourself to it. Don't you say that?"

Michael chuckled, thinking of his conversation with Cecilia.

"Yes," he said, "I do say that."

There was silence for a moment. Then Michael said, "There's one other thing. Forgive me. Maybe you can't tell me. I know it's someone else's story."

"George Jameson?"

"Yes. Heinrich had him killed, too, didn't he?"

"Yes."

"But last night—we didn't say *he* was praying for Heinrich."

"We didn't, because we couldn't. It wouldn't have been true."

"So, is he lost? I think he must have loved Cecilia once, so he can't be all bad. And I'm sure she loved him. They became one flesh. I'd hate to think there's no hope for him."

"I didn't say there's no hope for him, any more than I said it for Heinrich. I don't say that for anyone. There *is* something in him that is capable of nobler thought. Perhaps he may be brought to it. But… for now… he too has what he has chosen. George doesn't pray for anyone, not even for himself. Especially not for himself! But he *has* himself, to himself. And with himself and his own little fantasies it seems he is so far marvelously content. As Heinrich is also content. Neither desires to be anything other than what he already is."

Michael shuddered.

They stood for a moment in silence.

Then Spee smiled, a brilliant smile that took Michael by surprise and lightened his heart.

"Now let's talk of happier things," he said. "We left the academy's house rather quickly. When you learn what's happened there, you'll understand why. Cecilia I took home immediately. She has to work this morning and she needed her sleep. But I decided to bring you back to your home at this moment, in the middle of the morning rather than the middle of the night, just as you noticed. And I did it for a special reason."

"Oh. More of the time and relative dimensions stuff that Andrea's clever friends explained?"

"Exactly. So I suppose you could be said to have lost a few hours. Or to have gained them. It depends on your point of view. It is, on the one hand, several hours later than it was, but you are only a few minutes older, so you might be said to have gained time. On the other hand, if something happened in those few hours that you particularly wished to experience, I suppose you would have grounds for complaint. Er—was there anything you missed that you were especially looking forward to?"

"Not so far as I know," Michael said.

"Good. I mean, I *could* get you back if you really needed me to, but mathematically it's complicated and one is generally recommended not to go back on one's own timeline if one can avoid it."

"Well that's quite all right, Father. Don't worry about it."

"Well then, as I said, there's a reason I brought you back here at this precise moment rather than another. There's one other thing you need to do, and I believe"—he glanced at the eight-day clock—"that this is just about the time to do it. But I think you'll find quite difficult, in some ways harder than confronting that fool in the academy. In fact I'm not sure you're brave enough for it if I leave you alone. So I've decided to stay with you here to see that you do it."

Michael's heart sank. What new challenge confronted him?

"Let me see," Spee said. "Tomorrow—Wednesday—is the day you take as your day off, isn't it?"

"Yes, it is."

"And I happen to know our friend Cecilia Anna Maria has tomorrow afternoon off, to make up for extra duty she did one morning last week. So here's the difficult thing you have to do. You have to telephone her and tell her that you are planning to come down to Exeter tomorrow morning on the 10.06 from Paddington, and you wish to take her out to lunch."

"But I've no reason to go to Exeter tomorrow."

"But you do. You are going down to Exeter to take Cecilia Anna Maria out to lunch."

"But she might not want to."

"No, she might not. But until you've asked her you won't know, will you? And indeed, if you don't ask her she won't have any choice in the matter, will she? So do get on with it, like the good fellow you are. I rather think she's at her desk now. You would *like* to have lunch with her, I take it?"

"Very much."

Spee shrugged, glanced at the telephone, then looked back at Michael and waited.

Under the gaze of his mentor, Michael, feeling as he couldn't recall feeling since he was about thirteen, picked up the phone and stabbed in Cecilia's office number.

"DI Cavaliere here."

"Cecilia, this is Michael."

"Michael! I'm so glad to hear you. Last night you were *splendid*."

"I was? Oh! Well… thank you! Actually I don't think I'd have got through it without you. Look, Cecilia, I hope you don't mind but I thought maybe I'd come down to Exeter tomorrow morning on the 10.06 from Paddington, and I wondered if perhaps I could take you out to lunch? I mean, just if you're free. I know you're very busy. I'll quite understand if—"

"Oh Michael, that would be lovely. Yes, please."

"You will?"

"Yes of course. The 10.06 gets in at 12.09. I'll meet you on the platform, shall I?"

"Oh!—I mean, yes, that would be marvelous."

"We'll have tons to talk about. I have to rush now because there are about three hundred things happening here at once. But see you tomorrow. I can't wait!"

"Yes, tomorrow."

"Bye, Michael."

"Bye, Cecilia."

He hung up and looked at Spee.

"Well now," Spee said, "that sounds like a woman who's really difficult to please."

There was a pause. It occurred to Michael that there was a certain incongruity in his having just been encouraged in this way by one who had spent his life as a celibate. Spee smiled, evidently reading his unspoken question. "There's a way to our Beloved through the renunciation of images, and a way through their affirmation. You and my friend Cecilia Anna Maria are, I think, called by the way of affirmation. Neither way is without its joys and neither without its cup of bitterness. And both must pass through the gate and grave of death. But of course they meet, in the end."

Michael nodded.

"There's one other thing," Spee said. "You've both heard the music of the heavens, the heavens that declare the glory. You heard it together. And if you allow yourselves to remember that music—and I hope you do—it will fill you with a divine longing—*Sehnsucht*, we called it in German—and if you are wise—and I believe you are—you will know you can never satisfy that longing in each other. But you can help each other be open to it. You can give each other joys that are only images of true joy but not less precious for that. Indeed, they're precious *because* of that, and become more precious when they're recognized as that." He smiled. "And now I must go. God bless you, Father."

"God bless you, Father."

For a moment the two stood looking at each other, and Michael found himself reflecting that for all that separated them—centuries, cultures, the divisions of Christendom, even life and death—still what they had in common, what bound them together, was greater.

Spee nodded. "Exactly," he said. "We are in the Beloved, and our sins are forgiven."

With a gesture of farewell, he turned upon his heel and was no longer there.

It's odd, Michael thought, but the fact is, after one or two times, you start getting used to people who apparate, just like you start getting used to anything else.

SEVENTY-SEVEN

Heavitree Road Police Station. The same day.

Whatever private wonders may come to us, life goes on. After all that had happened the night before, Cecilia had been obliged to get up as if it were any other day, water her plants, take Figaro (the heroic Figaro!) for his walk, give him his breakfast, and go to work.

But by the time Michael telephoned, she was already in the middle of a highly unusual morning. To begin with, at 9.15 a.m., who should have arrived at the Heavitree Road Police Station but one of the two Assistant Chief Constables of the Devon and Cornwall Police. He summoned everyone available and announced that Superintendent Hanlon had resigned. An acting superintendent had been appointed: he was being drawn from the West Midlands and would arrive on Thursday. In the mean time, everyone was to carry on with his or her responsibilities. The assistant chief constable himself would be taking over the superintendent's office for the rest of the day and most of tomorrow, should any command decisions need to be taken.

In the buzz of speculation and conversation that followed these announcements, Cecilia—not normally one to be lacking in opinions on any subject or backward in expressing them—might have been perceived as unusually silent and incommunicative. She was not so perceived, but that no doubt was because others were too eager to express their own thoughts and opinions about what had happened to feel any sense of loss at being deprived of hers.

The truth was, of course, that in view of all that had gone on during the previous night, Cecilia suspected that she knew quite well why the superintendent had resigned. But like Hamlet's confidants she also felt constrained lest by some "ambiguous giving out" she might indicate what she knew of the matter, and be pressed for more on the subject than she was willing to give.

So she remained silent.

Still, she was not left simply to let the new arrangements pass her by. A quarter of an hour or so after Michael's telephone call she received a summons. Detective Inspector Cavaliere was to present herself to the assistant chief constable in the superintendent's office at 11.00 a.m.

Cecilia did not receive this notice without trepidation. Had Superintendent Hanlon left some parting accusation against her? She couldn't remember who it was who'd said he knew nothing against himself but was not thereby justified: but whoever it was, she reckoned she knew exactly how he felt.

She arrived at the superintendent's office at the appointed time and was immediately admitted—a pleasing change, she had to admit, from the normal practice of the previous occupant of that chair.

"Good morning, Detective Inspector. Please sit down."

"Good morning, sir. Thank you."

"Detective Inspector, the chief constable received two communications from Superintendent Hanlon this morning, both carefully dated and timed. One, dated this morning at 6.30 a.m., was his letter of resignation. The other was also dated this morning, but at 6.15 a.m. In other words, Superintendent Hanlon seems to have been rather careful to make clear that this letter represented his taking action in a certain matter *prior* to his resignation, and therefore while he still had authority to do so. Do I make myself clear?"

"I think so sir."

"Do you have any idea what this matter in which he took action was?"

"No sir."

Her heart leapt into her in mouth as she spoke. As he left, had Hanlon thrown a grenade over his shoulder? Demanded her resignation or suspension?

"Well, I'll tell you. He says that the transfer of Detective Sergeant Verity Jones to Barnstable was made in error, and that she is to be re-assigned immediately to this station. Since, as he goes to such trouble to make clear, he gave this instruction while he still had authority to do so, the Chief Constable and I are inclined to implement it. Does that meet with your approval?"

Cecilia's surprise at this was so complete that for a second she simply gaped at him open-mouthed.

"Yes sir. Detective Sergeant Jones is an excellent officer and we can really use her here."

"Good. That's my impression too and seems to be the feeling of every one of your colleagues I've spoken to. Now, there's a second thing in the letter, and this is the particular reason I've called you in. Superintendent Hanlon also recommends that DS Jones be assigned to work with you and assist you in your cases. Does that seem to you like a good idea?"

"Yes sir, it does. DS Jones has already worked with me on a few cases and I've found her assistance invaluable."

"Good. Then thank you, Detective Inspector. That assignment will be made."

"Thank you sir."

Cecilia stood for a few minutes in the corridor outside the superintendent's office considering what she'd just heard. Whatever

James Hanlon's faults had been, it seemed that at the end he'd tried to do the decent thing.

Father Spee had said Hanlon wasn't wholly bad. He'd also said that in time she might begin to feel more forgiving towards Hanlon. And now, it seemed, she actually did. Not *completely* forgiving, but certainly more forgiving than before.

So in that too, it seemed, Father Spee had been right.

Despite the cliché, it is not only bad news that travels fast. By the time Cecilia got back to her own office, it seemed that everyone in the station knew that Verity Jones was coming back.

Verity herself reappeared with her cardboard boxes that afternoon, to be greeted by an enormous piece of lardy cake on her desk from Mrs. Wyatt and a "Welcome Home" banner made by Joseph strung across it.

SEVENTY-EIGHT

Andrea and Rosina Cavaliere's house. The same day.

That evening the Cavaliere family had much to talk about. Cecilia mentioned that Michael Aarons was coming to Exeter tomorrow to take her out to lunch.

"Papa," she said suddenly, "you don't mind, do you? I mean, he's your friend."

Andrea, hardly expecting to be thus appealed to as one *in patria potestate*, shook his head. "Why on earth should I mind? Mama and I want you to be happy. Michael is a decent, honorable man."

It occurred to him that the implications of his answer went rather beyond having lunch.

But then, wasn't that true of her question?

"Well I for one am glad to hear it," Mama said, helping herself to more *spaghettini con salsa di gorgonzola e salvia*, "I was beginning to think he'd never get round to it. He's been fancying you for months—I've seen the way he looks at you."

Cecilia raised a quizzical eyebrow, but said nothing.

"I'm only referring to the fact that he thinks you hung the moon. Nothing more than that!"

Cecilia gave a half smile and sipped her wine, but still said nothing. Mama sailed on.

"Mind you, I can understand *why* he's been slow. For one thing he thinks he's too old for you. But that doesn't matter. Papa was fourteen years older than me."

"There's no need to rub it in," Papa said. "Anyway, what do you mean, 'was'? I still am."

"I was trying to be tactful," Mama said.

Some people have an extraordinary idea as to what constitutes tact.

"Well," Cecilia said, "Michael's only eight years older than me."

"There," Mama said, "that's nothing at all."

"How do you know he's eight years older than you?" Papa asked.

"I sort of... looked him up." Cecilia colored slightly.

"Looked him up, did you?" Papa said, "That was extraordinarily forward of you, young lady."

"Yes Papa, it was. I can't imagine where I learnt such behavior. When I was a child my education must have been sadly neglected."

He nodded. "Yes, it must have been. That's probably it."

"Poor Michael will be hung up on a lot of things, though." Mama was not about to be distracted from her own line of thought. "I'm sure one reason he hasn't done anything about it before is because he thinks you won't be interested. Michael's one of those genuinely humble men—there aren't many of them about—who really can't imagine how any woman he thinks attractive could possibly think he is. And then, being a priest he'll worry that he'll be letting God down if he puts *you* off God by doing the wrong thing. Oh yes, he'll definitely need some careful handling."

"Mama, for God's sake, I'm not going to *handle* him. I'm going to have lunch with him."

"Of course, dear. Sorry."

But Mama clearly had more to say. Andrea watched with amusement as his wife struggled to keep her thoughts to herself and failed.

"The thing is," she said, "men pretty well fall into two types. There's the self-centered egomaniac type who think the universe can go to hell in a hand-basket so long as they get what *they* want. There's a lot like that. You married one. And then there's the antique Roman hero type who always thinks he's got to sacrifice himself and give up anything *he* wants for the sake of everyone else. Michael's definitely that sort. My guess is, if you can just persuade him you *don't* need him to be a Roman hero all the time, he'll be an absolute sweetheart."

Andrea did his best to keep a straight face.

She'll be designing the wedding invitations next.

"And you can stop smirking, Andrea Cavaliere. You know very well I'm right."

"Yes dear."

I wonder which sort she thinks I am?

But then, as Rosina bent to recover her napkin, which had fallen to the floor, Cecilia winked at him.

He winked back.

As for the question as to which sort he was — perhaps that was best left until later.

Seventy-Nine

Heavitree Road Police Station.
Wednesday, 27ᵗʰ May. 10.00 a.m.

The phone on Cecilia's desk rang — it was Joseph, with good news. His endless, patient inquiries regarding the size-twelve boots had at last born fruit.

"In fact, I rather think we might have nailed it."

"Great!" Cecilia said. "Verity and I will be with you in just a few minutes."

A mail order firm in the north of England had sold a pair of size twelve Danner Desert Acadia military boots — just one pair! — last month. The boots had been dispatched to a purchaser in Exeter and the vendor could — and did — furnish the police with a name: William Saunders. Exeter address.

But that was not all. That name, when run through the police data base, at once produced a match: a man with two convictions for assault and three for burglary in the north of England, all of the latter with similar MOs to the Cumberland House break-in, save that they'd happened while the occupants were not at home, and so had not resulted in any violence.

So far so good.

"But if Saunders has all these convictions against him," Cecilia said, "surely we have his DNA on file. And if we have his DNA, and he's really our man, why didn't our search turn it up?"

"Ma'am, we *do* have his DNA on file. But for some perverse reason just that section of the Forensic Science Service database happened to be down on just the day we ran our sample through. They tell me they were upgrading the software. But of course nobody thought it worthwhile bothering to tell us we hadn't actually covered everything. I ran it again this morning, and guess what, now we've got a match."

Cecilia swore. "I can't believe I'm hearing this."

"I'm afraid it's the truth, ma'am. But I do think we've found your killer. Well, identified him, anyway."

"And so do I. Good for you, Joseph! We'll deal with what went wrong later. For now, Detective Sergeant, I need you to come with me. We're going to make an arrest on suspicion of murder. Joseph, notify them upstairs, will you? Tell them as a matter of urgency to circulate Saunders's description, just in case we don't find him at his address. For God's sake let's get this man off the streets."

"Yes, ma'am," Verity said. "*Fiat iustitia, ruat caelum!*"

"The trouble with a classical education," Joseph said to his computer screen, "is that nobody ever really recovers from it."

"Actually that wasn't classical, it was seventeenth century English jurisprudence," Verity said.

"Oh, go and arrest somebody, will you?"

EIGHTY

A little later the same morning.

The address was in Burnt House Lane, and it did not take them long to find it. Cecilia's car was unmarked, and of course neither she nor Verity were in uniform, but something about their approach must have given them away, for before they had even reached the front door they heard a door slam at the back of the house followed by the sound of pounding feet.

"He can't get far that way," Cecilia said. "It's a blind alley. Still, contact the station and ask for back-up. He's here and he's resisting arrest. Then cover this end for me. I'll go down the alley and keep an eye on him."

"Ma'am, be careful. He might have a gun."

"I don't think so. He's violent but there's no indication of firearms in his MO. You just call the cavalry."

"Yes, ma'am."

Cecilia entered the alley past an old-fashioned ironmonger's on the opposite corner from the house. She walked slowly. There was no sign of anyone so far as she could see—and nowhere to hide. After about twenty meters the alley curved to the right, and she could not yet see to the end. Presumably her quarry was there. She continued to walk, keeping to the left so as to have maximum visibility as soon as she came to the curve. Ah, that had to be him—down at the far end, a large fellow in a blue windcheater.

As she approached, he saw her and dived into an entrance at the side of the last building on the left. She continued to walk. No sign of him. She was almost there—within a few meters, balanced lightly on her feet, centered, ready for him should he leap out at her—when she heard footsteps behind her. She whipped round.

Damn! She hadn't realized there was a way round the back. He'd used it to get past her, and was now pounding away up the alley. Within seconds he'd disappeared round the bend.

Damn, damn, damn. She started after him with little hope. She was fast, but he had a thirty-meter start. There was no way she could catch him before he was up to the main street, with a dozen directions available.

She could still hear his footsteps—

A loud clang and a sound of clattering metal.

And no more footsteps.

What on earth had happened?

She ran to the bend, and was greeted by the sight of their man down on the ground, apparently unconscious amid a mass of metal dustbins, with DS Verity Jones kneeling over him. By the time she reached them, Verity had cuffed him. As Cecilia approached she could see some of Verity's curls had flopped forward and were hanging over her eyes: which was to say that by the standards of Miss Perfect she was looking positively disheveled.

"I hope I didn't hit him too hard," she said.

Cecilia looked at a large bruise ripening on the victim's forehead.

"How on earth did you give him *that*?"

"A dustbin lid, ma'am. He was going flat out and he was a quite large and I didn't really know how to stop him. So I grabbed one of the lids and just sort of stuck it out as he went by and he ran into it. You don't think I used unnecessary force, do you?"

Cecilia bent over and checked him. His pulse was strong. His eyes were starting to open. As he regained consciousness, she looked into his face. This was not a criminal mastermind of whose capture one could be proud. He looked broken, brutal, and frightened. She suspected he was on drugs and stole mainly to feed a habit. And though he must be held accountable for what he'd done, after what she'd heard last night she knew that a far greater guilt than his had led to the murder of John Stewart Cox, and that there was one who must therefore pay a greater accounting.

She heard an approaching siren. The cavalry was on its way.

She stepped away and surveyed them both: the prone captive well over six-and-a-half feet tall and broad in proportion, his feet clad in the Danner Desert Akadia boots that would turn out, she did not doubt, to be size twelve; and standing over him his captor, slim, fair, and diminutive by comparison.

"Unnecessary force?" she said. "No, I don't think anyone's likely to say that."

A police car, lights flashing and siren blaring, swung into view. Passersby stopped to watch as PCs Wilkins and Jarman got out and ran to the scene.

"Good morning," Cecilia said. "I seem to remember you two were the first on this case, so what better than that you're here at its end? DS Jones, you were the one that actually captured this man — indeed, if it hadn't been for you, he'd have got away — so you should make the arrest." She turned back the two PCs. "You two can take him to the station."

She watched as Wilkins and Jarman hauled their prisoner, now conscious and muttering imprecations, to his feet. She waited while DS Jones formally arrested him and issued the caution.

Sirens and flashing lights heralded the approach of two more police cars. DS Sims and Sergeant Stillwell emerged from one, Constables Jewell and Langdon from the other.

"Good," Cecilia said. "You've all arrived at just the right moment. We've just arrested this man, William Saunders, on suspicion of the Cox robbery and murder. He was in the house behind us immediately prior to his arrest, and I've reasonable grounds to think it may contain evidence. I want you to designate the place a crime scene, affect an entrance, and send for Scene of Crime Officers. Be careful not to contaminate anything."

"Yes, ma'am."

She watched as the four officers went about their business. Then she went back to the car and got in. After a few minutes Verity joined her.

"That was terrific, Verity," she said. "I let him fool me when I followed him down that alley, and I meant what I said just now — if it hadn't been for you he'd have got clean away."

"Thank you, ma'am."

"Don't mention it. Now, I'm going back to the station and I'm going to drop you there. You draft the initial reports on this and I'll look them over tomorrow. Make sure you draw attention to the breakdown in communication over the DNA."

A call came in on Verity's personal radio — DS Sims from the house. Cecilia could hear him from where she sat behind the wheel.

"Verity, tell DI Cavaliere we're being careful like she said, and we're not touching anything till the SOCOs arrive, so we haven't been able to confirm serial numbers yet, but I thought she'd want to know that as soon as we opened the front door the first thing we can see across the hall's a Samsung widescreen TV and a Dell Laptop that look like they *exactly* fit the description of Cox's stuff."

Cecilia gave a nod and for a moment took one hand off the steering wheel to make a thumbs-up sign, which Verity passed on.

Sims's call completed, Cecilia drove in silence for several minutes.

Then she said, "We can interview Saunders tomorrow. That will give plenty of time for him to have a lawyer present. Let's see if CDS can get him someone good. I want us to do this one right—but I'll tell you something about it now, for your ears only. I'm quite sure Saunders did the killing and the robbery, and I'm pretty sure CPS can make that stick in court. But I've also good reason to think Saunders was put up to it by someone from the Academy for Philosophical Studies."

"So you really don't think it was a robbery gone wrong, ma'am?"

"No. That's just what we were supposed to think. But once Saunders and his lawyer realize we've got him dead to rights, I hope he'll talk. If his defense plays it right, his cooperating with us will help him in court a lot more than not cooperating. That's one reason I'd like him to have a good lawyer."

The academy was no more, at least for the present, and its king rat was down and out to an arm of justice rather longer and more powerful than that of the Devon and Cornwall Police. But the king rat had certainly made use of lesser rats, and there would be no harm in giving them a little heat, if it could be done.

"All right, Verity. Is there anything else you think I should be doing about this?"

"I don't think so, ma'am."

"Well in that case, after I've dropped you at the station I'll leave. I'm supposed to have the rest of the day off, and this time I intend to take it. I'm going home to change, and then I'm meeting someone for lunch. A friend. A man. And my mobile will be turned *off*, airplane mode, so it'll be no use anyone trying to get hold of me."

"Oooh! A date?"

"I think so… To tell you the truth, I'm not quite sure. I'll tell you when it's over."

"Yes ma'am."

They drove on for several minutes, each engrossed in her thoughts.

Then Verity said, "Ma'am?"

"Yes, Verity?"

"I could truthfully tell Joseph I kicked ass today, couldn't I?"

"Oh yes, Detective Sergeant Verity Jones. You can truthfully say you kicked ass."

Eighty-One

Exeter St. David's Railway Station. The same day. 12.09 p.m.

The train from Paddington was on time and Cecilia spotted Michael as he was getting off it. He was wearing a royal blue sweater, a cream open-necked shirt, and light khaki pants.

It was the first time she'd seen him not in clerical dark gray or black. She thought how nice he looked. And how young.

He turned, caught sight of her, and smiled.

It occurred to her that she loved the way he smiled.

"Hello!"

It occurred to her she also loved the way he said hello.

For God's sake, woman, get a grip.

"Hello!" she said.

She could hear herself. She was nervous. She was actually nervous.

The public address system announced loudly that this train was now going to Penzance.

Well, good for the train.

As he approached she held out her hands and he took them. She stepped closer, meaning to kiss him on each cheek as she'd done when greeting him on other occasions. But then at the last minute something in her intention changed, or he moved, or she remembered something she'd nearly done once and then not done and then later wished she *had* done, or — for whatever reason, she kissed him on the mouth instead.

It was certainly not the longest or most passionate kiss in history. But then, neither was it perfunctory or brief. It was, at first, a little shy. But when it was over Cecilia knew that nothing would be the same again. She was no longer nervous. And yes, Verity, this was definitely a date.

Still holding her hands, he looked at her, and she returned his gaze, not without a little gentle amusement. For a few seconds his expression suggested he could scarcely believe what had just happened, then, as he accepted it *had* happened, a delight he hardly knew how to deal with, and finally a valiant effort to get hold of himself.

"Cecilia Anna Maria," he said at last, more or less calmly.

She smiled at him. "Father Spee called me that."

He smiled back. "I already knew it was your name. I looked you up on the Internet ages ago. I've always thought it was a beautiful name. But I rather think Father Spee made me brave enough to use it."

"Did you indeed? Looked me up on the Internet. That was very forward of you, sir."

"Yes, I suppose it was rather." His voice was light and happy.

He relinquished her hands and she fell in beside him, tucking one arm through his. They started to walk back along the platform toward the exits.

"So how long have you been in love with me?" she said.

He looked thoughtful.

"It's been coming on so gradually I hardly know. Maybe from the time someone told me how well Detective Inspectors are paid — *much* better than Archdeacons. Yes, definitely since then."

"So by way of inflaming your ardor perhaps I should point out we're due for a raise."

"That's wonderful. I'm sure I'll love you more than ever." He considered. "How much more will depend, naturally, on how big the raise is."

"Well, naturally."

They walked on a little further.

"Still," she said, "you were a bit slow doing anything about it."

"Yes, I suppose I was." His voice changed. "I didn't think—I mean, I couldn't imagine anyone as wonderful as you would be interested in someone like me."

"Well, for the avoidance of any further confusion, let me point out that *if* you knew anything about anything, which you obviously don't, you'd have noticed some time ago that I adore you."

"Really?"

"Yes. Really."

"Oh."

They walked a few meters further.

"Still," she said, "I must admit I was a bit slow too. I've known for ages I wanted to be with you, but you're a priest, and I've grown up with priests being off limits."

She looked sideways at him. He was shaking his head and smiling.

"Oh," she said, laughing herself, "of course I knew Anglicans have different rules and I was always sure you liked me. But still I thought you couldn't possibly be thinking about me the way I was thinking about you, and I was afraid I'd spoil it."

"*Thinking* about you?" He stopped walking, and turned to face her. He was still smiling, but she now saw there were tears in his eyes. "Oh Cecilia, I can hardly *stop* thinking about you. I am so hopelessly in love with you. It makes me happy just to be with you, to hear you talk, to see the way you laugh with your eyes. Although I must confess I'd like... I *ache*... to hold you..."

"Then why don't you?" she said softly, and made it easy by stepping close to him.

Doors were slamming along the length of the train.

Very probably their second kiss was also not the longest or

most passionate in history, but it surely rose dramatically in the ratings, and when it ended and Cecilia stepped back from it, she was breathless.

It took them both a minute to recover.

Again she tucked her arm in his and again they set off towards the exit.

"By the way," she said, "do you have the slightest idea how we're going to make this work?"

"Not the foggiest," he said.

"Me neither," she said.

They walked for several more minutes in contented silence, then—

"Well," she said, "having got all that sorted out, perhaps we should turn our thoughts to more serious matters. On the phone yesterday, didn't you say something about lunch?"

"Absolutely," he said.

Author's Note

In presuming to write about the Infernal City, or hell, one is aware of entering into and therefore drawing on a long tradition, beginning with Homer's descriptions of the underworld and the psalmist's pictures of Sheol, continuing through Virgil and Dante and John Milton, on through Jean Cocteau's wonderful film *Orphée* and the writings of C. S. Lewis, and most recently (at least in my reading) in Morgana Gallaway's *Inferno*. Evidently, I have drawn to a greater or lesser extent on all these. Equally evidently (I hope) my intention is to write fiction, not furnish information about the afterlife. That said, I would offer one qualification: destined though I believe we are to be partakers of the divine nature, I also believe that it is possible for us to refuse that destiny if we insist on doing so. To that extent, and insofar as I attempt to portray that reality, I would claim that my fiction is based on fact.

I am also, of course, not furnishing information about the defense arrangements of the United States and Great Britain. So far as I know, the last actual Peacekeeper missile was removed from alert on September 19, 2005. Although it is true that on occasion the United States Air Force has deployed from bases in the United Kingdom (as, for example, in the bombing of Libya in 1986, with the permission and encouragement of then Prime Minister Margaret Thatcher) I do not believe that Peacekeeper missiles were ever deployed in Great Britain. R.A.F. Harlsden and its role in western defense is entirely a fiction.

Father Friedrich Spee von Langenfeld, S.J. (1591-1635) is, by contrast, a historical figure, and his noble and pivotal role in ending the persecution of witches in the seventeenth century is, I believe, more or less as I have described it.

About the Author

Christopher Bryan is an Anglican priest and C. K. Benedict Professor of New Testament *emeritus* at The University of the South. He was born and grew up in London, and is a some-time Woodward Scholar of Wadham College, Oxford. He is the author of one previous novel, *Siding Star*, and several non-fiction books, including *Render to Caesar*, *The Resurrection of the Messiah* and *Listening to the Bible*. He and his wife Wendy now make their home in Sewanee, Tennessee, and Exeter, England. Find out more at www.christopherbryanonline.com or at his author's page at Amazon.